This time the sympathy, or had along? Either way, this was a good idea ...is hands. His fingers e~ ... ..an's would and brushed across her lip~.

'ust all nk

He kissed her again, a deeply sensuous kiss, and his hands caressed her neck and shoulders. He touched her breasts, lightly and through two layers of fabric, but it was enough, and Jenna felt both a shiver of pleasure and a stab of claustrophobic panic. She stiffened and caught her breath sharply.

"Do you want me to stop?" he asked, his voice husky.

"No," she said, but faintly. *Yes. God, yes.*

"Just tell me," he said. "*Now* would be a good time."

"No." She was glad he had asked, though. She wasn't about to be raped by Barbara Raymond's killer. No, she wasn't afraid of what he would do, but of what he could make her do—or feel. She didn't want to be hurt again as Patrick had hurt her.

Praise for Linda Griffin

Seventeen Days

by

Linda Griffin

To Julie Mackennan —
Happy reading!
Linda Griff

Seventeen Days

Cover Art by *Tina Lynn Stout*

The Wild Rose Press, Inc.
PO Box 708
Adams Basin, NY 14410-0708
Visit us at www.thewildrosepress.com

Publishing History
First Vintage Rose Edition, 2018
Print ISBN 978-1-5092-2296-4
Digital ISBN 978-1-5092-2297-1

Published in the United States of America

Dedication

To Anna Kalina, the kindest of readers

Acknowledgements

Thanks are owed to A for the inspiration;
Fran and Kathie, sisters, friends, and first readers;
and editors Nan Swanson and Windy Goodloe.

Chapter One

Light sparkled on the cool green water of the harbor. On the second day of bright sunshine after a week of rain, everything had a special, clear brilliance—the sky very blue; tall green grass, the meadow scattered with flowers. Against the sky and the ocean rose the clean, graceful shapes of fishing boats. The waves, the salt-fresh wind in the trees, and bird songs were the only sounds in the wonderful stillness. The entire scene had a soothing calm that eased Jenna's disappointment over her first sight of the house.

She headed back down the path to appraise it again. It was nothing like the enchanted palace of her dim childhood memories, but it wasn't so bad. The building appeared to be structurally sound, and it was certainly big enough for her to live comfortably in alone. The exterior needed paint badly, and she could see shingles loose and missing on the roof. The stepping stones she had jumped on when she was four or five were buried in long grass, which left bright drops of moisture on her shoes.

The steps needed repair, but the porch was still firm, and someone had swept it recently. She had

1

played here for hours as a child—how could the space have been so small? The screen door was rusty, and one hinge was very loose. She had been given a small brass key, but the door was not locked.

Inside it was cool and dim, most of the windows shuttered. She opened two of them, letting in the sunlight and fresh air. Except for a few cobwebs, the sparsely furnished living room was in good condition. A bucket strategically placed under a leak in the hallway was half full of water. In the kitchen, water stains were clearly visible on the ceiling. The room held only a small refrigerator, old gas stove, double porcelain sink, and too little cupboard space. It retained a little of the coziness she remembered from childhood, but she was dismayed by the lack of modern conveniences. After living in her efficient apartment in the city, could she manage without a dishwasher or a microwave? Jenna sighed. Such as it was, the house was now hers.

She walked into the master bedroom. The bed had been stripped, but her grandmother's portrait still hung on the wall. Her grandfather had slept in this bed until two years ago, when he relocated to Carroll City to be near his hospitalized wife. Now they were both gone, but something of their spirits remained, a mixture of her childhood memories and the stamp of their personalities on the furnishings.

They had been married for sixty years and still in love to the very end. Her own parents were still bickering fondly after thirty-two. Only she had failed. Patrick, who had once promised to love her forever, had left her for another woman. She could imagine no more humiliating failure.

Quick footsteps pattered on the porch, and a cheery, feminine voice called, "Hello!" She closed the bedroom door and hurried out to meet her first visitor. The woman on the porch was slender and girlish, with a dark ponytail and laugh lines around her eyes. She was carrying a covered dish. "Hi," she said warmly. "I'm Rosalie Hayes from next door. Welcome to San Ignacio. We've been expecting you for a couple of days."

"Hi," said Jenna. She reminded herself that in small towns everybody knew everybody's business. "I'm Jenna Scott."

"Pleased to meet you. I knew your grandfather. He was a lovely man."

"Yes, he was."

"I was very sorry to hear of his passing, but I'm glad somebody will be living in the house now. An empty house is like—oh, I can't think what!" She made a self-deprecating gesture, laughing at herself. "I brought you a casserole. It's hard to think about cooking when you're moving in and all."

"Thank you. You're very kind."

"I won't keep you, but if you need anything, holler. We're just up the hill a ways." She gestured, but Jenna couldn't see the house from the porch, only a stand of trees and the curve of a driveway. How remarkable to have a next-door neighbor out of sight. In the city, where you banged on paper-thin walls if the neighbors played their stereo too loudly, privacy was highly valued. Here she supposed she was expected to take an interest.

"Do you have children?" she asked because she couldn't think of anything better.

"Two," said Rosalie, smiling fondly. "A boy and a girl. You'll meet them soon enough. I hope Nancy doesn't make a nuisance of herself; she does sometimes. Listen, I know you'll be tired tonight, but tomorrow we'd like you to come up and have supper with us. It'll just be the family, me and Mike and the kids."

She hesitated. "Can I let you know later?"

"Oh, sure. When you get the phone hooked up, our number is one off yours, two instead of three at the end? Or you can just walk up any time."

"Thank you," Jenna said again.

"Sure. I hope you'll like it here. It's a good house."

"It needs a little work, though," she said ruefully, gesturing toward a rickety step.

"Yes," Rosalie said sympathetically. "Houses miss people; they go right downhill. But once you put things to rights, it'll be great."

"I should at least get the roof fixed before it rains again," she said, feeling tired and discouraged. "I don't suppose you'd know who I could call?" She didn't think a town like San Ignacio would run to yellow pages.

"Your best bet would be Rick Alvarez," Rosalie said at once. "He lives about half a mile down this road." She pointed to the narrow street that branched off the main road and ran along the edge of the water. "He doesn't have a telephone, but you can leave a message if he's not home. He's an excellent carpenter. Gabe Burrows will be up sometime tomorrow morning to hook up the phone for you. Don't let him scare you; his bark is worse than his bite." She put the covered dish in Jenna's hands and backed away, finding the best footing on the step as if she had done so many times before. "I hope we'll see you tomorrow."

"Thank you," she said yet again.

The house seemed even emptier when Rosalie had gone. Jenna carried her drafting table and two cartons in from the car and then returned to savor the view again. To the natives, the harbor was ordinary and practical, she supposed, the source of income from fishing and tourism. Her grandfather had gone out on a trawler almost every day of his adult life, and he had always been happy—as Rosalie said, a lovely man. Her memories of him were part of what gave the lines of hulls and rigging such poignant beauty.

She returned to the house and found a sketchbook and charcoal pencil in one of the cartons. Her wedding ring was in the box too, and she contemplated flinging it into the ocean. She had decided in the beginning that the only way to keep her dignity was to behave more like an adult than Patrick had. She put the ring in a drawer and returned to her view.

Nothing in life had ever given her as much joy as capturing on paper the beauty in ordinary things. Light, shadow, shapes—the spirit was always present somewhere. She spent a blissful half hour sketching boats, the wharf, the bait house, and the trees that hid the neighbors' house. Finally a distant white cloud with a gray edge reminded her roofs could leak. Fixing up the house seemed a daunting prospect, but she knew she would feel better once she made the first step toward action.

Rosalie had said Alvarez, the carpenter, was only half a mile away, so she decided to walk. Even if he wasn't home, a stroll along the shore on a lovely, sunny afternoon would be a pleasant diversion. Asking a stranger to repair her roof couldn't be any worse than dealing with the surly apartment house manager.

The walk did lift her spirits. Birds twittered in the trees, and a profusion of unfamiliar blossoms lined the road. She might be out of place here, but it was a perfect place to heal a broken heart. She was almost there before she thought to worry about Rosalie's not very explicit directions. More than one house might lie roughly half a mile along this road.

Where the road started to turn back away from the water she found an open gate and a mailbox with ALVAREZ neatly lettered on the side. The house was small, but predictably in good repair. A gray Ford pickup was parked in the driveway. A small, dark-haired boy sat on the steps with his elbows on his knees and his chin in his hands, apparently disconsolate.

"Hi," she said. "I'm looking for Mr. Alvarez."

"Hi," he said. He didn't smile, but he got up at once and went into the house. Jenna slowly climbed the steps, unsure whether she should follow, knock, or wait.

A man appeared in the open door, wiping his hands on a rag. He stuffed it into the pocket of his jeans and held out a hand. "Hi. Rick Alvarez." He was about five ten, Latino, probably in his thirties, good-looking in a stern, unsmiling way.

"Jenna Scott," she said. His handshake was firm and impersonal.

"Bill Scott's granddaughter," he said with a knowing nod. He had a pleasant voice and no accent.

"Yes. Rosalie Hayes recommended you. The house needs a lot of work. I don't know if I can afford to do all the repairs right away, but I want to get the roof fixed as soon as possible."

"I'll give you a fair price," he said matter-of-factly. "I could come by tomorrow and at least give you an estimate."

"I'd appreciate it," she said, relieved to find the transaction so easy. He didn't growl like the apartment house manager.

"Is it okay if I bring my boy? It's a school holiday."

She hesitated, dismayed. If she said no, she might have to find somebody else. He didn't seem to notice her hesitation. "Yes," she said. Would she be expected to entertain him? She didn't know very much about children and was in no mood to begin learning. He was what—six or seven? He hadn't come back out, and she remembered only his dark eyes and down-turned mouth. "He didn't look very happy," she said.

Alvarez smiled slightly, not enough to soften his face, and said, "He's sulking. It won't last long."

"Ah," she said. She didn't ask why. He seemed friendly enough, but not very inviting. A man who lived apart from his neighbors and without a telephone was not seeking easy intimacy. "I'll see you tomorrow," she said and took a step backward.

"I'll come in the morning if I can," he said. His tone suggested it could not make very much difference to either of them. Only in a small town.

The sense of having accomplished something gave her enough energy to carry the rest of her belongings inside and make up the bed. She uncovered Rosalie's casserole and glanced around automatically for the microwave. She would have to buy one later, next time she was in Carroll City. The house had electricity, which it hadn't when she visited as a child. The stove was ancient, and it took her a while to figure out how to light the oven with a match. At least the matches, kept in a stoneware box, were dry.

The casserole smelled and tasted delicious, with chicken, cheese, noodles, and a rich, creamy sauce. She sat at the kitchen table and sketched the Alvarez house from memory while she ate. She wasn't very good at portraits, but she put in a small figure on the steps. A sad little boy with big, dark eyes and his father's strong cheekbones.

She lay awake for a long time in her grandparents' bed, staring at the ceiling, too tired and keyed up to relax. She had thought the house would feel familiar and safe, but it only felt strange. What if she couldn't live here after all, even for a short time? What would the people here think of her? They had been kind so far—because she was Bill Scott's granddaughter? What about Gabe Burrows, whose bark was worse than his bite?

Chapter Two

Tuesday, February 12 (Lincoln's Birthday): Allied forces open combined land-sea-air barrage against Iraqis in Kuwait—largest battlefield action to date.

As usual, things looked a little better in the morning. She drank coffee without cream, ate a stale doughnut, and made a shopping list. She had brought only a few groceries and no perishables. The electricity had been turned back on a few days before, but she hadn't been sure the refrigerator would work. It did; she would survive.

As she backed out of the driveway, she could see the Hayes house, hidden by trees from the house but visible from the road, a neat white bungalow with bicycles in the yard. She took the half-familiar road into town. The entire business district of San Ignacio covered only a few blocks. She parked in front of Sam's Grocery and went in. The store was a single square room, clean and bright and well organized. A long counter was equipped with a scale and an old-fashioned cash register. A big blond man was seated behind it, chatting amiably with two young people, a slender, dark-haired boy and a chunky blonde girl in shorts and a halter top. They all stopped talking and turned to stare at her.

In the city she would have ignored them and

searched the shelves for what she needed. She reached back in her memory and produced an image: entering this store with her hand in her grandfather's, shyly responding to the greetings of the owners. She remembered a big man with a white mustache, called Grocer Sam to distinguish him from his fisherman son, and his pretty, curly-haired wife. Her grandfather had treated her to ice cream, and she had lingered over her choice of flavors, savoring the anticipation.

"Hi," she said to the three at the counter. "I'm Jenna Scott."

"Bill Scott's granddaughter?" the owner said, holding out his hand. "I'm Jim Kelly, and this is my daughter Heather. Have you met Larry yet?"

"No," she said. She was surprised by the friendly interest of the young people, so unlike the resentful indifference of city kids.

"Larry Hayes," Kelly said. "Your next-door neighbor."

"Hi," she said. "I met your mother."

Larry unaccountably blushed. He was a good-looking boy with a definite resemblance to Rosalie, approaching his full height at sixteen. Heather was younger, pink-cheeked and ponytailed, with a soft, lilting voice. They excused themselves politely and left the store, Larry striding ahead, and Heather hurrying to catch up, swinging a bait bucket.

"Kids," Kelly said fondly. "He's taking her fishing, and you'd think he'd given her diamonds."

"I'd prefer fishing, myself," Jenna said. "Diamonds are overrated."

He laughed, although she was quite serious. "Are you settling in all right? Need some supplies?"

"Yes and yes." The present ambience of the place blended with her memories, and she held out her list, remembering her grandfather doing the same thing. It was apparently still the right thing to do. Kelly looked over the list and gathered things from the shelves as he talked.

"When we heard Bill had left the house to his granddaughter, we were afraid you would sell to outsiders or summer people." Apparently he didn't consider her an outsider, even though nobody here could possibly remember her childhood visits. "Are you planning to stay awhile?"

"I hope so." If she had run away from the city to hide, where would she run if she couldn't make it here? At least here she would never run into Patrick or his skinny blonde girlfriend. "I'll be working on a book, if I can concentrate in all this beauty."

"Ah, you're a writer," he said, his tone a mixture of satisfaction that he had categorized her and disapproval of so impractical a calling.

"No, an illustrator."

"Ah," he said again, apparently mystified. Perhaps Bill Scott's granddaughter was an outsider after all. He added up her purchases on the cash register and packed them in an open-topped cardboard box. She scanned the counter displays, which included gum and candy but no cigarettes. "Anything else?" he asked. She hesitated, tempted by the Hershey bars, but resisted.

The door behind her opened abruptly, and a voice boomed, "Hullo, Jim Kelly!"

"Morning, Violet." The person who marched up to the counter was in no way like her name. She was a tall, beefy woman with a tangle of streaked blonde hair, dressed in overalls and a green flannel shirt. "Violet Hopkins," Kelly explained to Jenna. "This is Bill Scott's granddaughter."

"Of course it is!" Violet announced in her deep, rough voice. "Who did you think I supposed she was? The Queen of Sheba? Hullo, Jenna Scott! Heard you hove into town last night. Now, listen here. Anybody doesn't treat you right, you let me know. We don't put up with any nonsense in San Ignacio."

"Violet is on the town council," Kelly explained.

"Hell, I am the town council!" she corrected and then laughed. Her laugh was as deep and rich as her speaking voice.

"I'm pleased to meet you," Jenna said as soon as she could get a word in. She held out her hand, and Violet enveloped it in both of hers.

"We're all pleased to have you here! Bill Scott was a good man—none better. Your daddy was a corker too, if I remember. Well, Jim Kelly, are you giving this little gal everything she needs?"

"Everything she asked for," he said. "Couldn't say about what she needs." He winked at Jenna.

"None of that talk!" Violet boomed. "Now, listen here. I'm having a barbecue on Saturday. I have a grocery list as long as your arm, and I want a notice put up, too. Everybody in town is invited, and if I don't see you both there, I'll know the reason why."

"You know we'll be there," Kelly said. "Nobody can resist your ribs."

"I know *you* can't," she agreed. "I 'specially want you to come, Jenna Scott—good chance to meet everybody."

"Thank you."

"Never mind thank you, just be sure to show up, no later than twelve noon. Now, Jim, I ain't in a hurry, so you go on and see she gets those supplies loaded in the car. What kind of car is that?" she asked, but didn't wait for a reply. "It's a real pretty shade of blue anyway."

Kelly lifted the box and followed Jenna out to the car. "Violet's a mite loud," he said, "but she has a good heart."

"I'm sure she does," she agreed. With such colorful characters as inspiration, maybe she *should* write a book.

When she got home, a van was parked in the front yard, and Rosalie was talking to a tall, gaunt man with fiercely bushy eyebrows. "Hi!" Rosalie called as she got out of the car. "You're just in time. Gabe is here to hook up your phone."

"Good morning, Miss Scott," Gabe Burrows said sternly. He sounded as if he suspected her of illegal activities.

"Good morning," she said, holding out her hand, which he ignored.

Rosalie took a few steps away, ready to leave. "Can we count on you for supper tonight?"

"Yes, thank you," she replied, although she hadn't given it much thought. She didn't see any point in being unsociable. She had met more people in San Ignacio in less than twenty-four hours than she had in the apartment building in as many months. Rosalie was probably the nicest of the lot, and she would prefer to be on good terms with the neighbors.

"We'll eat at six thirty," Rosalie said. "Come early and we'll talk."

"Okay," Jenna agreed.

"That woman has too much time on her hands, if you ask me," Burrows grumbled. He started up to the house, and she followed, both amused and intimidated. "Now, I can put the phone somewhere else if you want," he said grudgingly, apparently used to city folks' nonsense. It was in the kitchen, where she remembered it had always been, but now the instrument was more modern, with cheery yellow plastic and a push-button dial.

"This is fine," she said, and he set to work, quickly and silently, while she put away the groceries. When he was finished, he handed her a local phone directory, dated 1987, and presented a work order for her signature—a simple printed form, no carbons.

He said, "We'll send you a bill first of the month. Any problems, give us a call."

"Thank you, Mr. Burrows."

"The name's Gabe," he corrected. "I knew your grandfather." As he gathered up his tools, he nodded toward the stained ceiling and said, "Been neglected awhile, I guess."

"Yes, my grandmother was ill for a long time. Rick Alvarez is going to give me an estimate on the roof."

"Alvarez," he said disapprovingly. He said something else, which she hoped she had misunderstood, under his breath and went out. Jenna followed as far as the porch and called, "Thanks again, Gabe. Goodbye." He didn't reply, but he waved as he drove out. In a place like San Ignacio, even the town curmudgeon was a friendly sort.

She convinced herself she shouldn't start work on the book only to be interrupted by the carpenter and instead made a batch of cookies to take to Rosalie's, coming as close as she could to her grandmother's recipe. The cookies were in the oven, filling the room with warmth and a rich, chocolaty fragrance, and she was scrubbing the sink and counter when she heard a car turn into the driveway.

It was Rick Alvarez and his son in the gray pickup, the bed piled with plywood sheets and paper-wrapped bundles. The little boy got out first, clutching a coloring book and a box of crayons, but stayed close to the pickup while his father lifted a ladder out of the back. Alvarez wore black jeans and a black T-shirt with a tool belt around his hips like a modern-day gunslinger.

Jenna stepped out on the porch and let the screen door slam behind her so he would know she was there. She wasn't sure what to say to him. The beauty of dealing with the apartment house manager was that once you had convinced him something needed fixing, he was responsible for hiring the repairman and making sure he did the job properly. She wasn't sure she was up to the responsibility of being a homeowner.

"Good morning," Alvarez called. He beckoned the boy to follow him up the steps. "Danny, this is Miss Scott. My boy Danny. I don't think you met formally yesterday."

"No, not formally," she agreed. "Hi, Danny."

"Hi," he said softly. He seemed much more cheerful than the day before, but stayed close to his father.

As they passed into the house, Alvarez took notice of the loose screen door hinge, but he said nothing. He followed her into the kitchen, the sound of his boots on the hardwood floor echoing in the nearly empty rooms, and she pointed out the leak in the hall and the stained ceiling.

He studied the stain for a few seconds before he nodded curtly and said, "I'll go up and take a look."

"You're not going to take your son up on the roof, are you?" she asked. The idea of anybody walking around up there made her a little queasy.

He gazed at her as if he wondered why she cared, but all he said was "No." He bent and whispered something to the boy and gestured at the kitchen table. "Okay?" he asked Jenna.

"Oh, yes, sure." Danny climbed up on a chair and laid out his crayons with careful precision. Alvarez headed back outside, and she was left with this strange, quiet child. She had no idea what she should say or do. Danny, oblivious, began to color.

She was saved by the bell—the oven timer chimed, and she hurried to take out the cookies. They smelled wonderful, even if they were not exactly like her grandmother's. She offered one to Danny, and he hesitated and then took it shyly. "Thanks," he murmured.

"Would you like a glass of milk with that?" she asked. He shook his head and bent over his work. Jenna resumed her scrubbing. She heard sounds from overhead but couldn't tell what he was doing. A sudden crash made her jump, and she glanced quickly at Danny, who kept coloring, unconcerned. More loud noises followed, and she realized Alvarez was tearing off loose shingles and throwing them to the ground. She started to go out in the yard and remind him they had agreed only on an estimate, but she didn't want to see him on the roof. What if she startled or distracted him and he fell? It had been so much easier to go off to work and let the manager deal with everything.

When the cookies had cooled a little, she began packing them in an old cracker tin. The screen door banged, and Alvarez strode in. "The roof's not so bad," he said conversationally, leaning in the doorway with his thumbs hooked in his tool belt. "If you want to come out, I'll show you what needs to be done."

Jenna hesitated. It would be the cautious, sensible, homeownerly thing to do, but San Ignacio was a small town, and this man was practically a neighbor. She might as well be honest at the start. "I wouldn't know what I was looking at," she confessed. "All I need to know is how much it will cost and how long the job will take."

He took a pen and a small spiral notebook out of his pocket and scribbled a few figures. "It won't take long. I can do it right now, if you like. I have enough shingles in the pickup."

"How did you know…?"

"Didn't," he said. "But I got a good deal on the shingles. Do you know Jeff Tanner?"

"I don't know anybody here," Jenna said.

"Anyway, he had them left over…I think they'll be a good match." He tore the page out of the notebook and handed it to her. It didn't exactly constitute a contract, but the final figure was encouragingly low. If the roof leaked, she would know where to find him.

"All right, let's do it," she said. "These cookies are fresh out of the oven. Would you like one?"

"No, thanks. I'll get to work." He started to leave and turned back just as she handed Danny another cookie. He raised an eyebrow.

Danny, with the cookie halfway to his mouth, caught the look and said, "*Gracias.*"

"In English," Alvarez corrected.

"Thank you, Miss Scott," Danny said dutifully and bit into the cookie. He seemed unembarrassed, but she wondered if his father wasn't a bit of a bully to correct him in front of her.

"This is California," she said. "We at least know *gracias.*" He didn't answer, and his face was unreadable. He left the house, banging the screen door again, and Jenna finished putting the cookies in the box. She didn't want to entertain the boy, and apparently it wasn't necessary, but now she was a little curious. "What are you coloring?" she asked, but made no effort to see his page.

"Trucks," he said.

"Oh, you like machines. I like to draw buildings, myself." He looked up and regarded her gravely, and she felt as if she needed to prove herself. She retrieved her sketchbook from the bedroom and showed him the rendering of the Alvarez house. He gave her a small smile and pointed to the figure on the steps.

"That's me."

"It's supposed to be. It's not very good."

"I like it," he said, making a simple, straightforward statement of fact, not meant as a compliment or a request, one artist to another.

"Would you like to keep it?" she asked. "I can always draw another one."

"Yes, please," he said. His father—or someone— had taught him manners. She tore off the page, and he laid it carefully beside his row of crayons. "The house is sad," he said and gave her a shy look, shaded by his beautiful eyelashes. "Houses are sometimes," he explained.

"Yes," she agreed. "But my house isn't. It's getting a new roof, and it smells like freshly baked cookies."

"But I like trucks the best," he said and picked up a blue crayon.

A loud thump on the roof made her jump. As long as the Alvarez men were working, she might as well join them. The technical drawing required for the book she was illustrating was not as enjoyable as sketching the harbor, but the project would pay for the groceries. She could at least start the preliminary sketches at the kitchen table. Consciousness of the carpenter working above her head kept her a little on edge, but she disciplined herself to work steadily.

She and Danny had worked in companionable silence for some time when a car door slammed. Danny immediately dropped his crayon and was out the front door like a shot. Vaguely alarmed, she followed as far as the front window.

Danny joined Alvarez at the pickup, and they sat on the open tailgate and dug into a large sack for sandwiches and thermoses. Jenna glanced at her watch, which showed exactly noon. When she looked up again, Danny was talking animatedly. His father nodded gravely a couple of times and then suddenly smiled, a nice, warm smile that broke up the too serious lines of his face. She felt a pang of longing for the lost dream of Patrick as the father of her children. No, she would not think of Patrick here; he had lost the right to enter this peaceful haven, even in memory. She returned to the kitchen and briskly set about making herself a sensible, nutritious lunch.

Danny didn't come back after lunch. Alvarez climbed back onto the roof and began pounding in nails. He had passed the stage of throwing shingles to the ground, and it was safe enough for Danny to play outside. She could hear him running back and forth in the front yard, making engine noises. Not so long ago she had played there herself, inventing grandiose plans for a future full of castles and unicorns. She was too restless to settle down to straight lines and careful angles, so she decided to give the house a thorough cleaning. Real physical work was therapeutic, and her spirits lifted.

She was mopping the kitchen floor when Danny came running in, skidded to a stop at the door, and announced, "Miss Scott, my dad says come see." She had been so busy she hadn't noticed when the sounds on the roof stopped. She leaned the mop against the wall and followed Danny out to the porch.

Alvarez was holding the screen door open, and he pulled a screwdriver out of his tool belt and gestured at the loose hinge. "No extra charge," he said.

"Thank you," she said. Danny tugged on her hand, and she followed him into the yard. She shaded her eyes and stared up at the roof, but it looked exactly the same in the front. Danny led her around to the side of the house, and she could see where a sizeable area had been reshingled. The new shingles made the rest appear a little faded by comparison, but the job was neatly done and made her feel altogether better about the prospect of rain.

When she had admired the roof to Danny's satisfaction, they returned to the porch. Alvarez had finished with the screen door and was testing the ricketiest step with the toe of his boot. "Ought to put new boards on one of these days," he said, but didn't sound as if he meant to pressure her.

"Come in the house, and I'll write you a check," she said. They followed her into the kitchen, and Danny put his crayons back in the box while his father again leaned in the doorway. Danny showed him the sketch of their house, and he took the page without comment and studied it briefly before he handed it back. Jenna dug her checkbook out of her purse and filled in the amount from memory, but hesitated over the name. "Rick" didn't seem formal enough for a check. "Is it Richard?" she asked.

"Enrique," he said, and she flushed a little under his cool gaze, as if she should have known. His eyes were dark and deep-set, his lashes as thick as Danny's. She wrote his name and signed her own in her usual no-nonsense style. He didn't even check to see if the amount was right—he knew where to find her if there was a problem—and folded it. "Thanks," he said, slipping it into his pocket.

"I appreciate your doing the job so quickly," she said. "It was nice meeting you, Danny."

"Bye, Miss Scott," he said blithely. She wanted to say something else, ask something, make conversation like a small-town neighbor instead of a customer, but nothing occurred to her. For some reason, she felt more socially inadequate than she had since she'd sported braces in the fifth grade.

She followed them out to the porch and watched Alvarez lift the ladder back into the pickup bed while Danny climbed into the cab. As he was about to join Danny, he asked, "Will we see you at the barbecue?"

Ah, Jenna thought, that's what I should have asked!

"Yes," she said, and he nodded and turned away, as if her answer didn't matter much.

"Bye!" Danny called again. He waved at her as the pickup swung onto the road, but Alvarez never looked back.

Jenna returned to the kitchen and finished mopping the floor. The task took only a few minutes and, still feeling energetic, she decided to explore the small backyard shed. It was locked, but the wooden jamb was rotten, and the door flew open with one hard tug. More work for the carpenter. She would have to make a list and figure out a budget. An old, rusty push mower was nestled among the cobwebs. She found a can of oil on her grandfather's workbench and set to work. When she was finished, the mower squeaked a little, but the blades spun freely. Mowing the lawn was far more satisfying than any kind of housework. A yard was one of the things she had missed in the apartment. The sun and fresh air and the satisfaction of visible progress made the job seem easy. The place was beginning to look lived in.

When she had finished the lawn, she went inside and took a bath—there was plenty of hot water—and dressed for dinner at Rosalie's. She chose stonewashed jeans and an embroidered blouse, hoping to strike a balance between small-town casual and company formal. She couldn't remember if Rosalie had been wearing any makeup, but decided pink lipstick was safe anywhere.

A little after six she climbed the hill, carrying the tin of cookies and a handful of daisies from the front yard. Taking coals to Newcastle, perhaps, but having her hands full made her feel less shy.

She approached the house from the back, and Rosalie opened the kitchen door before she reached it and called, "Hi, neighbor!" She wore a terrycloth apron and sandals, but was otherwise dressed as she had been in the morning. "Come on in. I'm making the salad." She took the daisies and put them in a water glass, somehow more appropriate than any vase. "How sweet," she said, as if daisies didn't grow all along the road.

Jenna held out the cracker tin. "I made some cookies. I thought the kids might like them."

"Chocolate chip," Rosalie said approvingly. "My favorite. Nancy will like them, and Larry will eat anything. Growing boys are incredible to cook for; they'll inhale anything, as long as there's lots of it." She turned back to the kitchen table and began rapidly chopping celery. Jenna was dazzled by such skill. The kitchen was warm and bright, with a window above the sink and the walls painted pale yellow. The sink and the square butcher-block table were old-fashioned, but a new refrigerator, a four-slice toaster, and a modern stove brought it up to date. The cabinets looked newly finished and definitely more spacious than hers.

Rosalie noticed her looking and opened one of the cabinets. The handles were carved wood, and the inside was painted white. "Aren't they beautiful?" she asked. "Rick made them for me."

"Rick Alvarez?" Jenna asked stupidly.

"Yes. He's really an artist." Head bent over the salad bowl again, Rosalie asked slyly, "What did you think of him?"

Alarm bells rang in Jenna's head. Rosalie was

hoping for gossip; whatever she said would be repeated. "He did a nice job on the roof," she said indifferently. Rosalie looked up, one eyebrow raised, and she fended off another question with, "It seems strange that he doesn't have a phone."

"Not everybody here does. He's very good-looking, isn't he?"

"Mm," she said noncommittally. "Danny's a nice kid. Where's his mother?"

"Dead. They say…" She glanced nervously toward the door and, changing her tone, called, "Nancy, come on in."

A young girl with dark braids and blue eyes bounced in at once. She was about ten and had the bold stare of the uninhibited.

"Were you eavesdropping?" Rosalie asked. "Here, make yourself useful." She tied an apron around the girl's waist and handed her a knife, and Nancy began cheerfully mangling a tomato. "This is our new neighbor, Miss Scott."

"Hi. Did you make that blouse?"

"No," she admitted. "Do you like it?"

"I can sew. My mom says I make very neat stitches."

"Yes, you do," Rosalie agreed. "But it isn't polite to brag. Where's your brother?"

"Watching the news," Nancy said disapprovingly. "I'm sick of this old war."

Jenna was disappointed. The Hayes family had a TV set, and San Ignacio was not proof against the ugly reality of the Gulf War. "Me too," she said.

"Danny's mother was murdered," Nancy said, returning to the subject she had overheard.

"Don't repeat gossip," her mother said.

"Everybody at school knows it," Nancy insisted.

"Everybody at school should stick to their reading and arithmetic. The only thing anybody knows about Mrs. Alvarez is that she died before they moved here." Her expression suggested she would love to say more in the absence of little pitchers with big ears.

Nancy shrugged and changed the subject again. "Are you married?" she asked Jenna.

"No," she said, ignoring the technicality of her pending divorce. "But if I had a daughter, I'd like her to have braids and blue eyes and know how to make neat stitches." Nancy stopped butchering tomatoes to stare at her, openmouthed. She was speechless for a change, and her mother laughed, delighted.

Rosalie took the knife out of Nancy's hand. "That's enough tomato, I think," she said. "Why don't you go set the table?"

"I hate setting the table," Nancy complained. "It's boring."

"Do it anyway. It'll be good for your soul."

"Things that are good for your soul are always boring," Nancy said, but she gathered a handful of silverware and clomped loudly into the dining room.

"I understand you ran into Larry at the store," Rosalie said. "He went on and on about it."

"About me?"

"He's at an impressionable age. Glamorous older women."

"Glamorous?" Jenna shook her head. "Now I'm afraid I'll disappoint him. I'd better be brilliant at dinner."

"Don't worry about it. He and Mike will probably

talk fishing. What did you do in the city?" Jenna could see where Nancy had gotten her directness. She did her best to explain technical illustration, and the girl returned for plates and stopped to stare at her curiously. She opened her mouth to ask a question, but a gesture from her mother stopped her. Still, it was only a matter of time before everyone in town would know everything about Jenna, including the fact that her husband had left her.

While Rosalie was describing the intricacies of her family—she was a fourth-generation San Ignacian and had married her second cousin—the back door banged open, and a sunburned blond man entered. He had left his oilskins and boots in the shed but smelled of fish and salt water. He gave Rosalie an absent-minded kiss without touching her and stared at Jenna with frank interest.

"This is my husband, Mike," Rosalie said unnecessarily. "Mike, our new neighbor, Jenna Scott."

"Bill Scott's granddaughter," he said. He held out his hand, but thought better of it. "I'd better take a shower," he said and left the kitchen. He reminded her so much of her grandfather that she couldn't help smiling.

Almost immediately, Larry burst through the door. "Mom," he started and stopped when he saw Jenna.

"What, honey?" Rosalie asked, tossing the salad.

He blushed. "Nothing—uh, nothing. When's dinner?"

"In a few minutes. See if Nancy has the table all set."

"She's—oh, never mind." He stalked out.

"Kids," said Rosalie, shaking her head. "God bless

'em."

As if on cue, Nancy came back and announced, "Mom, Larry pulled my hair."

Unperturbed, Rosalie asked, "What did you say to provoke him?"

Nancy giggled, and her mother handed her the salad bowl. "We'll eat as soon as Dad's out of the shower," she said.

"What can I do to help?" Jenna asked. She was beginning to feel self-conscious standing in the kitchen with nothing to occupy her hands.

"Adult conversation," Rosalie said. "To keep me sane." She opened the oven door and took out a juicy, browned roast, which smelled wonderful. She was the sort of old-fashioned housewife Jenna could never hope to be, with a talent for cooking and sewing and child rearing. Maybe if she were more like Rosalie, Patrick would have…

She mentally shook herself. Rosalie wanted adult conversation. "Is fishing still San Ignacio's main industry?" she asked.

"Pretty much. It's not like it used to be, of course, but tourism has picked up, so we get along."

"Don't you hate that, though? Tourists everywhere?"

"Oh, they don't bother us much, and they spend a lot of money. It's bad sometimes in the summer, but not this time of year. Violet has one cabin rented right now—some woman from L.A. I haven't met her yet. I hope she's not as pushy as some of those folks." Again Jenna blessed her grandfather's memory for making her less of an outsider than "those folks."

Rosalie began a detailed account of past pushy

behavior, but was interrupted by Nancy, who announced, "Dad's out. I'm hungry. Can I sit next to Miss Scott?"

"If you mind your manners," Rosalie said and handed her a basket of rolls.

The dining room was small but nicely decorated, with burnished oak furniture and figured cream wallpaper. Mike and Rosalie sat at opposite ends of the table, and Nancy claimed the seat next to Jenna, leaving Larry across from her. Fortunately he only seemed interested in talking fishing with his father. She didn't want to play the role of sophisticated woman of the world, even to a sixteen-year-old's taste.

Nancy tried to win Mike's attention by teasing Larry about Heather Kelly, but her brother gave her a disdainful glare, and the fishing talk continued. Rosalie said, "You did hear about Violet's barbecue?"

"Yes, I ran into her at the grocery store."

"Isn't she great?"

"She's bossy," Nancy volunteered.

"If you can't say anything nice—" Rosalie warned.

"Well, she is," Nancy said, unabashed. "I think Miss Scott is really nice, don't you? Larry said…" Larry, distracted from fishing talk, glared at her, and she stopped talking, but not for long. "Larry and Heather, sitting in a tree, k-i-s-s-i-n-g."

"Nancy!" Rosalie's tone and expression made it clear she would brook no further nonsense. "These are not her best company manners," she said to Jenna. "Anyway, Violet throws the best parties ever. The food is always great."

"I'm looking forward to it," she said, although she wasn't sure she was. "Isn't it risky, planning a barbecue in February, though? What if it rains?"

"Oh, it won't," Rosalie said, but didn't explain her confidence.

"It wouldn't dare," Mike put in, apparently more aware of their conversation than she had realized. "Violet wouldn't allow it. You know, Miss Scott—"

"Jenna."

"Jenna—I went fishing with your grandfather when I was about Larry's age. He loved the sea, that man."

"Yes, he did," she agreed. She was a little disconcerted by his direct, interested gaze. If he hadn't been a happily married man, she would have said he was flirting, after he'd ignored her for ten minutes.

"He was a good man," Rosalie said. "Everybody here loved him."

Her eyelids stung. "Yes," she said. "I know how he felt about the sea. It is beautiful."

"And dangerous," said Rosalie.

"Beauty often is," Mike said, looking directly at Jenna. He *was* flirting with her, right under the eyes of his family.

She took a sip of water to cover her confusion and said, "This roast beef is wonderful."

"I'll give you the recipe," Rosalie said. Was she completely unaware? Or used to her husband's conversational style? Surely he didn't mean anything by it.

"I helped," Nancy put in, jealous of the visitor's attention.

"Nancy is a great help," her mother agreed.

"Too bad she's such a pest," said Larry. Typical family conversation, which she would now never have with Patrick, or perhaps with anyone.

Later, after she had helped Rosalie and Nancy with the dishes and followed the path back to her own door, Jenna decided she had been imagining things. Mike was only being friendly to a guest, and she must not let Patrick influence her to distrust all men.

Chapter Three

Saturday, February 16: Iraq's ambassador to U.N., Abdul Amir al-Anbari, says Iraq will use weapons of mass destruction if U.S. bombing continues.

Saturday dawned clear after two days of dreary rain—and the roof had not leaked. Violet Hopkins could probably control the local weather, Jenna reflected as she swept her porch in the early morning sunlight. She was looking forward to the barbecue with both pleasure and apprehension. It would likely be more fun than bar hopping with Patrick's co-workers, but she was painfully conscious of her status as the new girl in town, Bill Scott's granddaughter or not, and the object of much curiosity. At least she wouldn't be the only stranger; Rosalie had said the woman from L.A. was invited.

Rosalie had given her directions to Violet's place, and she set out a little after eleven to follow the road through town and up the hill to where the Hopkins acres spread impressively green and spacious across the landscape. A dozen cars were parked in the driveway and under the oak trees flanking the handsome two-story house.

She could hear a murmur of voices, punctuated by the shouts and laughter of children, as she got out of the car. She followed the sounds beyond the house and took in at a glance the scope of Violet's hospitality. Trestle tables and benches were grouped near the house, and four grills sizzled under the supervision of the hostess herself, grandly outfitted in a voluminous chef's apron and a hat that resembled a pink Viking helmet. As many as twenty children were running and shrieking, apparently involved in a game of tag. Adults and teenagers stood or sat around the patio and lawn, chatting and watching the exuberant youngsters.

At first Violet, busy with cooking instructions, was the only person she recognized. She was at a loss as to how to approach this group of friendly strangers until she spotted Mike and Larry Hayes and Gabe Burrows standing with a tall blonde woman, and not far beyond them, Rosalie perched on a picnic bench talking with two other women.

She started in their direction but was intercepted by a small body hurtling into her, closely followed by a running tag player. She disentangled herself from the first child, a little blond boy. His pursuer, flushed and giggling, was Nancy Hayes.

"Hullo, Miss Scott," she caroled, grabbed the hand of the little boy, and raced back into the game.

"Are you all right?" asked a masculine voice behind her. "Little monsters never look where they're going." She turned and found, not the vigorous young man the voice had suggested, but a thin, white-haired gentleman with a cane. "Miss Scott, I believe," he said, holding out his hand. "I'm David Hopkins." His handshake was firm and warm. Jenna, who would never have guessed the loud, bossy Violet had a husband, much less such a courtly one, was momentarily speechless.

"I'm pleased to meet you," she managed finally.

"Did the boy knock the wind out of you?" he inquired. "Would you like to sit down?"

"No, I'm fine," she assured him.

"Let me take you around and introduce you to everyone," he offered, holding out his arm. "You can't have met many of us yet."

"Thank you," she murmured. She felt a little bemused but greatly comforted. She did not have to ride into battle without a champion.

Everyone she had already met—the Hayes family, Gabe Burrows, Jim and Heather Kelly, Rick and Danny Alvarez, and Violet Hopkins—greeted her with casual friendliness. She was introduced to so many people the names and faces blurred together. Jim Kelly's wife, Monica, was an older version of Heather, plump, blonde, and very sweet. Jenna liked her at once and hoped they would be friends.

The tall blonde woman who had been chatting with Gabe Burrows and the Hayes men had drifted on to another group and was introduced as Barbara Raymond, the renter from Los Angeles. She had short, blunt-cut hair, wide gray eyes, and a plunging neckline. She seemed nice enough, shaking hands warmly and giving Jenna a direct, interested gaze, but she was intimidatingly beautiful.

Everyone was so kind Jenna's nervousness vanished, and within a few minutes of her arrival she was seated at a picnic table with Rosalie, Monica, and two other women whose names she had immediately forgotten, laughing and chatting. Much of the conversation was about children, but she didn't feel excluded. Enticing aromas drifted toward them from the grills, and people began to line up to fill their plates. Before she could think about joining the line, Larry Hayes approached the table with a plate in each hand, set one in front of his mother, and offered the other to Jenna.

"Oh, thank you, Larry," she said, genuinely pleased by such generous behavior from a teenage boy she barely knew. The plate was piled with barbecued ribs, baked beans, corn on the cob, pineapple chunks, and buttermilk biscuits. She didn't think anybody except a teenage boy could eat so much food at one sitting, but she didn't want to hurt his feelings by suggesting she might be better off with a more modest portion. Such a neighborly impulse should be encouraged. He headed back to fill another plate for himself, and she claimed a fork from the center of the table and sampled the beans.

"Violet sure knows how to feed a hungry crowd, doesn't she?" Rosalie said. "I could fast for a week after one of her shindigs."

"This is great!" Jenna exclaimed. The beans were hot and sweet and surprisingly flavorful. She tried a chunk of pineapple. Was it actually fresh pineapple, or did the fresh air and camaraderie make even canned fruit taste better? Maybe she *could* eat all this food.

She had a mouthful of buttered biscuit when Danny Alvarez, running and laughing with the other children, tripped and fell. His father was standing with two other men, a little apart but apparently interested in their conversation—not that she was watching. She knew he had seen Danny fall, but he didn't react immediately. He watched while Danny picked himself up and then walked slowly toward him. Danny wasn't crying, but he had skinned his knee a little. Alvarez bent down to put an arm around his shoulder and spoke to him briefly. Danny nodded and almost immediately broke away, eager to get back in the game. Alvarez called a final word of caution after him and turned away. He was nearer the tables than he had been before and instead of returning to the men's conversation he drifted over and sat down on a corner of the bench across from Jenna, where he could watch Danny play.

"Danny's a pistol," Rosalie said, and he gave her a grateful smile.

"He's a good kid," he agreed.

Rosalie and Monica continued talking about their children as if there had been no interruption, but Jenna, who had not felt excluded before, found herself constrained by an odd shyness. She was relieved when Larry came back with another plate, piled with twice as much food. She gave him a smile and, gesturing toward her own plate, said, "Delicious."

"Yeah," he said and blushed. She could see that he was pleased by her attention—sophisticated older woman indeed!—but something else had crept into his manner. It was not exactly a swagger, but he was clearly conscious of the presence of another male, against whom his masculinity must be measured. Instead of sliding into the seat at the end near his mother, he stepped over the bench to sit next to Rick, almost jostling him, and asked, in a deeper voice than she had heard yet, if anyone had seen the coverage of the latest Patriot missile launch.

Her nerves crisped as she listened. She couldn't bear hearing people talk about the Gulf War as if it were a football game. *Hooray for our side*, and people were dying. Larry, like so many others, was anxious for the ground war to begin. She managed to keep silent, eating her ribs and corn, until he expressed the age-old masculine fear that the war would end before he was old enough to join the fray.

"Thank God it will," she said. "War is not a game, Larry."

"I know," he said. "I'm not a kid." But he was; he was so incredibly young, and she could imagine what his mother must feel, hearing him talk about risking his precious, promising life.

"You wouldn't be a hero," she protested, unable to censor herself. "You would be cannon fodder." He bristled, ready to defend himself—oh, yes, no doubt he knew from movies what war was like—and she cut him off with, "You wouldn't have a choice. You don't know anything about it."

He grabbed his plate and stood up, pale and angry. "Neither do you," he said coldly and left with all the dignity he could muster.

An awkward silence, which Jenna was aware she was responsible for, stretched out until Rick said, "You're right, but he won't thank you for it."

"Fortunately, he isn't old enough to run off to prove you wrong," Rosalie said.

One of the women, whose name Jenna couldn't remember, laughed and pointed in the direction Larry had taken. "He's found a more sympathetic ear," she said.

They all looked, trying not to be obvious. He had joined the three men gathered around Barbara Raymond, and she gave him a welcoming smile.

"I heard she's from L.A.," Monica said. "Pretty enough, I suppose."

"Gorgeous," Rosalie said. "If you like that type."

"Her haircut is really cute," said one of the others. "We aren't the ones to judge, but she certainly attracts a lot of male attention. What do you say, Rick?"

Rick, put on the spot as the only man at the table, didn't hesitate. "She's too beautiful," he said. "Women like that are nothing but trouble."

"Ah, you knew that was what we wanted to hear," Monica said, laughing.

He shrugged and turned his back on Barbara Raymond. Jenna, who had thought he sounded perfectly serious, found herself meeting his eyes as the other women discussed Barbara's dress and shoes with great relish.

"Rosalie tells me you made her kitchen cabinets," she said.

"That's right."

"They're beautiful. I wish I could afford something like that."

"You could make better use of the space in your kitchen," he agreed. "If you like, I could measure and see what we could work out."

"I don't want to waste your time," she protested. She was afraid she was committing herself to something she couldn't afford, and for what? To make conversation with a man whose silence made her uneasy? Why? He was handsome, in a stern, off-putting way, but she had seen his tenderness with Danny and knew he was no ogre. She groped for another topic of conversation, but the weather was trite, the war had proved dangerous, and she knew nothing about him except his work. What could she ask about his work that wouldn't end up costing her money? "Oh, I meant to tell you the roof didn't leak at all in this last rain."

"Danny put your drawing up in his room," he said. "It was very nice of you to give it to him."

"He said he prefers trucks, though," she said and won a faint smile in return.

"Preferring trucks to boats is heresy around here," Monica put in, not having heard the context.

Aha, something she could ask him about. "Do you ever repair boats?" she asked.

He shook his head. "It's a different kind of work."

His indifferent tone made her ask, "Did you grow up around here?"

"No," he said. "Los Angeles."

That surprised her. He was more of an outsider than she was. "It's a lot different here," she said.

"Quieter," he agreed.

She could think of nothing else to say, but Rosalie rescued her by pointing out that he wasn't eating. "You'd better get in line before they run out," she said. "Everything is delicious."

"Violet never runs out," he said, but he got up and headed in the direction of the food.

"The beans are terrific," Jenna said. "What does she put in them?"

"The recipe is a secret," Monica said. "Molasses I'm pretty sure of, but I've never been able to duplicate it."

"Monica is an excellent cook too," Rosalie said. "Her pumpkin pie is to die for."

Monica waved a dismissive hand. "Anybody can make pumpkin pie," she said.

Jenna, who bought hers frozen, wondered if Patrick's new girlfriend could cook and if he would have stayed if she could make to-die-for pumpkin pie and baked beans like Violet's. A second later she decided she didn't care—or she wouldn't care. Would she have met women as genuine as these in Patrick's circle of friends?

Rick returned with a modest helping of ribs and beans. Apparently he hadn't come for the food. He had no sooner sat down than Danny came running and climbed up beside him. The game was breaking up as hungry kids headed for the chow line. Danny leaned against Rick and smiled shyly at Jenna across the table.

"How's your knee?" she asked.

"Fine," he said. He stretched a hand toward his father's plate, and Rick shook his head.

"Get your own," he said.

Danny looked toward the food tables, where some of the older children were jostling and laughing. "Come on," Jenna said on a sudden impulse. "I want more pineapple." She picked up her plate. Danny ran to join her and took her free hand with a confidence that surprised and charmed her. They joined the line, and Danny very quickly had a plate filled high with every variety of food available. He was obviously not a picky eater.

Violet, hovering over the grills, caught Jenna's eye and called, "Save room for dessert, now!"

"Dessert!" she exclaimed. "I think I've died and gone to heaven."

Danny laughed, delighted, as if he'd never heard the expression before. They returned to the table, and he dug in at once, with little regard for neatness or manners. Rick ruffled Danny's hair and said, "Thank you," to Jenna with more warmth than the occasion called for.

She almost said the outsiders needed to stick together, but she hadn't been made to feel like an outsider and didn't know him well enough to guess what he felt. He was certainly more a part of the community than Barbara Raymond, who was now eating daintily at a distant table, surrounded by admiring males.

Dessert proved to be chocolate cake with raspberry sauce. "We *are* in heaven," she told Danny after one bite. He grinned, but didn't finish his. Violet had started organizing games, and he was eager to join one of the children's races. Rick hung on to his arm long enough to get most of the chocolate and raspberry off his face before he let him go. He hadn't taken any dessert and shoved Danny's unfinished portion aside indifferently.

"Why don't you finish it?" she asked. "It's delicious."

"I don't like chocolate," he said.

"Heathen," she said at once. "Philistine."

The other women immediately chorused agreement with her, but it was to Jenna he gave his rare, dazzling smile. She felt as if she'd been blinded, but continued the joke by handing him a spoon. He good-naturedly sampled the sauce, but his verdict went unstated, as Violet chose that moment to announce the first race and the promised prizes.

Rick stayed at the table and watched until Danny won a large red balloon as third prize in the sack race, and then she didn't see him again for more than an hour. Not that she was looking for him.

After the games the musicians warmed up, and square dancing began. She didn't know how but caught on soon enough when first Mike Hayes and then Jim Kelly asked her to dance. They were both married, which didn't seem to matter at all in this gathering. Everyone danced with everyone else with no apparent jealousy or favoritism, although she did notice Larry watching with a sulky expression while Barbara Raymond do-si-doed with his father.

When she was tired of dancing, Rosalie suggested a game of cards. Jenna had never played canasta, but she picked it up quickly and enjoyed the friendly rivalry. Monica was the best player—Jenna began to think she was the best at everything—but they all had a good time, talking and laughing and scoring points.

The cards had been laid aside, and they were talking casually when Rick Alvarez reappeared with Danny asleep on his shoulder. "Aww," Monica said, and her hand rested lightly on Danny's hair. "Somebody's had too much fun."

"He loves to come here," Rick said. He glanced at Jenna, and she knew she should contribute to the conversation, but there was still something intimidating about him.

"Is that why you're here?" she asked and flushed at how blunt it sounded.

He gave her a curious look. "Mostly," he said. "Did you come for the food or to get acquainted with everyone?"

"Both," she told him. "The food was great, and I made a lot of new friends."

"Good," he said and nothing more, his expression as closed and forbidding as she had yet seen. He shifted Danny's weight, raised a hand in farewell to Monica, and turned to go.

"Good night," Monica called, and Jenna echoed her, feeling stupid.

The party was still going on when she made her excuses and headed home. It had been a good day, but she was tired. She swung into her own driveway with a strong sense of relief and homecoming.

She was a little afraid the stimulation of the party would make it hard to sleep, but after she had a quiet hour with a book and a cup of hot cocoa, she slept as deeply and peacefully as she ever had in her life.

Chapter Four

Sunday, February 17: U.S. and Iraqi troops clash in seven incidents along Saudi-Kuwait border.

Jenna woke up early to a crisply beautiful morning, took her steaming coffee and her sketchbook, and walked down the hill toward the harbor. The view was gorgeous. She sat on a rock and started trying to capture it. She was good at buildings and quickly sketched the pier and the boats and the suggestion of clouds in the sky, but the ocean was beyond her skills. It was beautiful in the early morning light, changeable and alive, its color as deep and dazzling as she had ever seen.

She caught her breath at the sheer beauty of it and reflected that if she had still been married to Patrick she would have missed this. If she had been married to anyone, she would be at home making his breakfast. She might have children like Danny or Nancy, but she wouldn't have this incredible view. Unless she was married to a man with the sensibility of an artist, who would admire the ocean with her—and no, she wasn't thinking of anybody in particular.

A single boat was visible on the horizon, the only sign anyone else was awake. It was Sunday, and even the fishermen were sleeping late. She enjoyed the peace and quiet for about twenty minutes before she noticed a stir down below.

Two men stood near the edge of the trees, looking down into the water. She couldn't see them clearly, but they seemed to be searching for something. She was both curious and resentful of the intrusion. The sound of their voices drifted up to her.

Her quiet interlude ended, she got up and returned to the house. The salt air had given her an appetite, and she made bacon and French toast and poured herself a tall glass of orange juice. Her kitchen was as peaceful as the harbor had been—until she heard a clatter outside.

She opened the front door, a little apprehensive, but the noise was only Nancy Hayes dragging a stick behind her along the stepping stones. Jenna went out on the porch to greet her.

"H'lo, Miss Scott." She sounded unusually subdued.

"Good morning. Did you come to visit me?"

"Uh-huh." She stood for a moment, digging the stick into the grass, before she said glumly, "Mom and Dad had a fight."

"I'm sorry. Have you had breakfast?"

Nancy considered the question as if it had unsuspected pitfalls. "Oatmeal," she said at last. She twisted a lock of her hair around one finger and gazed hopefully at Jenna.

"Come on in," she said, amused. "I'll make more bacon and French toast."

Nancy cheered up a bit. "Do you have maple syrup?" she asked.

"No," Jenna admitted, "But I have raspberry jam."

Nancy let the stick drop and followed her up the

steps and into the kitchen. She picked up a piece of bacon, took a bite, and then looked guiltily at Jenna.

Jenna had to laugh. "You might as well go ahead and finish my breakfast," she said. "It will only get cold." She started a fresh batch, but she wondered if she ought to feed another woman's child behind her back. If she were Rosalie, what would she want her to do? She had said not to let her be a pest. "Does your mom know you're here?" she asked.

"No," Nancy managed to say with her mouth full of French toast. "They went to church."

"You didn't go with them?"

"I wouldn't. I hate it when they fight and then pretend everything's okay."

"Mm," said Jenna, trying to sound sympathetic and not at all curious. "What about Larry—is he home?" Was Nancy old enough to be home alone? Perhaps in a small town like San Ignacio.

Nancy snorted. "He went to church. He *always* goes. Heather goes, so—*duh!*"

"Well, Heather seems like a nice girl. I can see why he likes her."

"He lo-o-o-o-o-ves her," Nancy corrected. "Yuck!"

"Just wait. You won't always think love is yucky." As soon as the words were out of her mouth, she realized she had taken the conversation in the wrong direction.

"Do you have a b-o-o-o-y friend?" Nancy asked, and before she could answer, "Is there any more orange juice?"

"In the refrigerator," Jenna said and almost held her breath while Nancy poured juice and gulped it down. But she hadn't forgotten…

"Do you?" she asked.

"Do I what? Do you like your bacon crisp?"

"Yes. Yum, I love bacon. Are you a good cook?"

"Not very," Jenna admitted.

"*Do* you have a boyfriend?"

"I only moved into town six days ago, remember?"

"But did you before that?"

"Oh, lots of them," Jenna said, keeping her tone light. "Haven't you ever liked a boy?"

Nancy started to shake her head and then said softly, "One."

"Aha. I knew you were a romantic at heart."

"I never wanted to *kiss* him," Nancy said indignantly.

"Of course not. You have plenty of time for that." Before she could say anything more, she heard the crunch of tires on gravel out front. "See who it is," she said. She began laying hot, crisp strips of bacon on a paper towel.

Nancy got up, ran to the front window, and then skipped right back and sat down. "Danny's father," she said and grabbed for the raspberry jam.

Jenna finished what she was doing before she reluctantly opened the front door. She couldn't remember what had been said at the barbecue. He had said something about the cabinets, but she was pretty sure she hadn't asked him to come by on Sunday morning to discuss them. Small town or not, this was a bit much, especially when he had been barely civil when he left the party.

She stood on the porch and waited while he got out of the pickup. She was cross enough to demand, "What are you doing here?" but waited for him to speak first.

"Morning," he said. He was wearing his tool belt.

"Hi," she said coolly.

"Looks good," he said, gesturing at the shorn grass. "Where's Danny?"

"Sunday school," he said. "I thought I could measure your kitchen before I have to pick him up." He seemed perfectly at ease and confident, but when she didn't respond, he slowed and added, "If it's convenient."

"Not really," she said. "I'm cooking breakfast. But as long you're here…" She turned and went back to the kitchen. He followed, saying nothing and again letting the screen door slam, which was starting to get on her nerves.

"Hi," Nancy said. "Miss Scott makes great French toast. Want some?"

"No, thanks," he said. "I'll just—" He held up a measuring tape. Jenna said nothing.

There was an awkward silence before Nancy said, "We were talking about *boys*."

"Ah," said Rick and started measuring the cupboards.

"I'm a romantic at heart," Nancy informed him.

"Good for you," he said.

"Are you?"

"No, probably not," he said, sounding a bit absentminded. He stretched toward the cupboard above the stove just as Jenna turned to get a plate, and they almost collided. "Sorry," he said and backed up to let her pass. Nancy giggled, and Jenna knew they had exchanged a look behind her back.

She slid more bacon onto the girl's plate and sat down to eat. She wished he would leave—he had declined food for himself, and breakfast was not a spectator sport. Living here, she would need to learn the fine art of setting boundaries she had taken for granted in the city.

Oblivious to her resentment, Rick said, "I could put a shelf here for a microwave if you'd like. What about a dishwasher?"

"No," she said, "I don't mind washing dishes in the sink." It wasn't entirely true, but a dishwasher would have to wait.

"Good view for it," he said, gesturing at the window. "That will give you more space for storage—I could put drawers here."

"This is starting to sound expensive," she said. Not to mention having him around for days at a time.

"It won't hurt to draw up a few plans and give you an estimate," he said. "No cost, no obligation."

"My mom lo-o-o-o-ves her new kitchen," Nancy said. "She said it was worth every penny."

"Word-of-mouth advertising," he said. "Nothing like it."

"Her cabinets are beautiful," Jenna acknowledged, "but I'm sure there are other things I should do first—updating the kitchen isn't my first priority."

"She doesn't have a boyfriend," Nancy put in.

Rick was writing down measurements and didn't even pause. "Was that a non sequitur?" he asked.

Nancy munched bacon while she considered this. "Not on purpose," she said at last.

Rick and Jenna exchanged an amused glance over her head. "A non sequitur is something that doesn't follow logically from what went before," Jenna explained gently.

When Rick finished measuring, he put his notebook away and left the kitchen without a word. The screen door banged shut behind him.

"He's nice," Nancy said, "but the—"

Jenna cut her off. "What did your mother say about repeating gossip?"

"It isn't gossip if it's true. Danny's mother is dead. Is your mother dead?"

"No. She's fine, thank you. She lives in Arizona with my dad and three cocker spaniels."

"I like dogs. We can't have one because of the—the whatchamacallits. They make Larry sneeze."

"Allergens?" Jenna suggested. She was waiting for the sound of the pickup leaving. She didn't hear anything, and through the window above the sink she saw Alvarez crossing the back yard. "Do you want any more bacon?" she asked.

Nancy shook her head and then remembered her manners. "No, thank you, Miss Scott." Jenna got up anyway and checked to be sure the burners were off as an excuse to see where he had gone. He was poking around the shed. She had said there were other things she needed done, but he shouldn't assume she meant to hire him to do them!

She started piling dishes in the sink, and Nancy helped by putting away the juice and the jam. Rick left the shed and disappeared around the corner of the house. Again she waited for him to leave, and again she heard nothing. Nothing in her city-bred experience made it acceptable for him to hang around, but their previous dealings didn't allow her to go out and say, "Get off my property. You're not welcome here," either. If she had been alone, she might have continued to wait and wish he'd leave, but Nancy was more curious or more gregarious. Appetite temporarily satisfied, she ran outside to see what he was doing.

Jenna followed reluctantly. Through the front window she saw him talking to Nancy. He had his notebook and pen out again, no doubt listing things he could charge her for. He and Nancy walked out of sight—not toward his pickup. She sighed in exasperation and went to retrieve her sketchbook.

She sat on the front porch with her feet on the loosest step—no doubt the repair was on his list—and sketched the path and the driveway and the pickup. Danny would have liked it. The pickup wasn't new and had a few dents in the tailgate, but it was clean.

Rick and Nancy rounded the corner of the house. "Your paint is peeling," Nancy told her.

"I know," she said. "It's an old house, and nobody lived here for a long time. What color shall I paint it?" She hoped Alvarez had understood the "I."

"Pink," Nancy said at once. "It's my favorite color."

"Pink is nice," Jenna agreed. "But maybe not for the exterior."

Nancy climbed up the steps to see what Jenna was drawing, but when she found only a boring pickup, she lost interest. "Okay, red," she said and resumed following Rick around.

Jenna flipped a page. Portraits were not her forte, but she began trying to capture his face. There was something foreign about him. Not unfamiliar, not threatening, but somehow off-putting. She was equally puzzled by his face and by her reaction to it. She was embarrassed to think his ethnicity might be what bothered her—after all, she had lived in California all her life.

He was attractive enough, but not classically handsome. By a purely Anglo standard, his nose was too broad, his jaw too prominent—but when she looked up to see him listening patiently to Nancy's chattering, she could see only that they were right for his face. By any standard he had lovely cheekbones and slender, expressive hands, and she had never seen such beautiful, dark hair. Why was he here? Why was he *still* here? Her sketch didn't do him justice anyway, and when he glanced up and caught her watching him, she busily shaded the background and turned another page.

Nancy was being a bit of a pest, but he didn't seem to mind. He pulled a paint scraper out of his tool belt and showed her how to remove the flaking paint around the window. She set to work with more energy than skill, making a lot of unnecessary noise, but Jenna supposed she couldn't do much harm. Once she was well into the job, Rick came up and joined Jenna on the porch. He glanced at her sketchbook, which now showed only Nancy's pigtails and glasses.

"I can do that myself," she said, gesturing toward the window.

"I know," he said. "But she likes to help. Don't pass up free labor."

"When do you have to pick up Danny?" she asked pointedly.

He checked his watch. "Not yet," he said. "Not so hard," he added to Nancy.

"You don't go to church?" Jenna asked.

"Not today," he said. He was probably Catholic. Did San Ignacio—named after a saint after all—have a

Catholic church? Uh-oh, she thought, remembering her high school fascination with Catholic boys—Mexican, Italian, Irish. He wasn't sitting too close, but it felt too close. On her property was too close. He wasn't dangerous, but on some level she *was* afraid of him—why? He was Danny's father, and Danny was a terrific kid, and she had seen the sweetness of the affection between them. Was she wary of all men in the wake of Patrick's desertion? Would she feel this if Jim Kelly or Mike Hayes were sitting here?

He glanced at her sketchbook, and she tightened her grip for fear he would take it out of her hands and look at the previous pages. She added bows to Nancy's pigtails and tried to get the exact shape of her mouth—wide, gently curved, with her mother's sensitive lips. "You do this for a living?" he asked.

She shook her head. "Technical illustration. I'm not very good at portraits."

"Technical illustration," he repeated and nothing more, and she was damned if she could think of a single thing to say about her work or anything else. The silence stretched out, and she wondered if it was as uncomfortable for him as it was for her. She at least had something to do with her hands. He was leaning forward with his elbows on his knees and his hands clasped. He didn't seem uncomfortable. The only sound was the scraping of paint.

She opened her mouth to say something, anything, out of desperation, and he started to speak at the same time. He stopped and gestured for her to go on with a faint smile. "How long have you lived in San Ignacio?" she asked.

"Three years."

"And Los Angeles before that? Did you do the same kind of work?"

"No," he said and then he stood up. He took the scraper out of Nancy's hand and showed her again how to free the loose layers of paint. He faced Jenna on the steps, but didn't come back. "I was a teacher," he said.

"Really?" She imagined him showing teenage boys how to do woodwork or auto mechanics as casually as he demonstrated paint scraping for Nancy.

"Yeah," he said, acknowledging her surprise. "I taught history."

"This is a big change, then," she said.

"It is," he agreed and abruptly changed the subject. "Jenna. Is that a nickname?"

"No," she said. "It's on my birth certificate." She stood up too, because a car was racing along the road. A white car with beacon lights on top—the local police.

Rick took a step toward his pickup and put the paint scraper back in his belt. An unusual energy was in the air, and she understood his response without knowing how she knew. He was a parent, separated from his child. There was unknown trouble, and his instinct was to go find Danny. An odd thing to feel when she had no children of her own, but she knew she was right. He headed for the pickup, but remembered to stop and give them a wave in farewell.

"'Bye," Nancy called, disappointed but not particularly surprised. She didn't seem concerned or even curious about the police car. She brushed paint dust off her hands and the front of her dress and came back up the steps slowly. Her face brightened when she saw what Jenna had drawn. "That's me," she said. She sounded every bit as pleased as Danny had.

"Yes," Jenna agreed and gave her a better look at the sketchbook. "Pretty girl."

"No," she said and, no doubt remembering what she had been told about compliments, added, "I mean— thank you. I wish I could draw like you."

"I wish I could sew like you," Jenna offered. And cook like your mother, she thought, and keep—no, she would not waste a minute of this beautiful day feeling sorry for herself. She sat back down and filled in details of the portrait under the subject's admiring eyes. She didn't have it quite right, hadn't captured Nancy's unique personality, but it didn't have to meet any critical standards. When she had done all she could, she tore off the page and gave it to the girl. "I should go wash the dishes," she said. "Do you want to help me?"

Nancy considered, torn between the lure of further conversation and distaste for boring kitchen chores. Jenna laughed at her expression. "Never mind," she said. "They'll keep." She was happier now that Rick was gone, freer. Why was he so hard to talk to, when he had been as friendly as anyone else in town? Maybe he was too damned good-looking. "Tell me about yourself," she suggested. "What do you like to do besides sew and scrape paint?"

Nancy giggled. "I don't like school," she said, "but I like to read."

"Good. What books do you like?"

"I'm reading one about a whaling ship," she began enthusiastically. She recounted the story to date while Jenna sketched what she hoped was a passable whaler.

"My favorite was *Black Beauty*," she said, and Nancy had read it too. The conversation was very satisfactory, and Jenna was feeling relaxed and

54

comfortable when the rest of the Hayes family returned from church. Nancy, all reason for resentment forgotten, ran off to join them.

Jenna went into the house and washed the breakfast dishes. When everything was tidy, she headed out to the shed and found a paint scraper of her own. At the risk of spoiling the girl's fun, she set to work, adopting Rick's technique. When the task grew tiresome, she decided buying paint would be more fun.

She drove into town. Judging by the dearth of parked cars and passersby, some businesses were closed on Sunday, but the tiny hardware store was open. To a city girl used to large home improvement centers, it was like a child's conception of a store, a hardware dollhouse. The door was open, and the overhead lights were on, but nobody was around. The only paint was a few cans of black Rust-Oleum and white exterior flat, but a display showed colors she could order.

She surveyed the choices. Here was no extravagant wealth of shades, and the colors had straightforward names, no "Pecan Cream" or "French Vanilla." She considered a pale green, daringly christened "Light Green," or the truly exotic "Almond" for the kitchen, which would have to wait until she knew whether Rick Alvarez would talk her into remodeling. Of course she could start right away with white.

"Hullo," a hearty voice said behind her, and she jumped. The speaker was a young man she remembered from the barbecue, but his name escaped her. He was a pretty good square dancer and had a cute, girlish wife. "Planning to paint?" he asked.

"Yes," she said. "I'm sorry; I've forgotten your name."

"Harvey Wells," he said. "Too many of us to learn all at once."

"Yes," she agreed. "You're Megan's husband."

"Right," he said, beaming. He gestured toward the paint display. "I can get you any of those colors in three days at the longest. Of course the big paint stores in the city have more choices, but we only carry the one brand." Carroll City was nearly two hours away—too far to drive for pastels with edible names. "See anything you like?"

"I guess I'll start with white," she said, "and maybe something for the trim." She studied the display.

"Take your time," he said. He sauntered to the small counter and busied himself with a pencil and paper.

Jenna flirted with Nancy's choice of red—the color called "Red" was the shade of old barns—and decided on a deep forest green, dubbed "Dark Green," for the exterior trim. Harvey looked up and smiled when she approached the counter. He wrote down the information, offered an opinion on how many gallons of each color she would need—he knew the house—and offered to carry the white he had on hand to her car. "Now, if you need help with the painting," he continued, "there's lots of kids who'll work cheap." He gestured at a bulletin board near the door, covered with bits of paper. "They don't do anything fancy," he said, "but they're all good workers. We take them down if we get complaints."

She wondered what Rick Alvarez thought of this low-priced competition, but she dutifully studied the board. The scraps held brief job descriptions— "painting, yard work, chores," said one—names, and in some cases phone numbers. Larry Hayes had a listing, but she doubted he would be interested in helping her paint after she had hurt his pride. His sister probably would, if she could be trusted. Ought she to offer to pay Nancy for scraping paint? Or save her pennies for whatever Rick might talk her into? "No cost, no obligation," he had said.

While Harvey was writing out a receipt for her, she glanced around the store. It held mostly tools of every description—rakes, hammers, screwdrivers, drills, paintbrushes, and so on—and generous supplies of nails, screws, and tape. Between the bulletin board and the counter was a narrow case labeled Local Artists. A quick survey revealed the sort of thing she would expect to find in any tourist-area drugstore—amateurish shell jewelry, watercolor cards with sentimental poetry, embroidered potholders and checkbook covers, and on a shelf by themselves a series of wood carvings with a surprising delicacy of detail. She picked one up—a kitten curled up in comfortable sleep—and found it light and smooth in her hand, the texture of the wood almost lifelike. She checked for a price sticker on the bottom. It was signed in neat capitals—E. Alvarez. *Enrique,* she thought and felt herself flush as Harvey approached to hand her the receipt. She put the kitten back on the shelf. So he *was* an artist.

She and Harvey carried paint cans out to stow them in her car. She was opening the trunk when Megan hurried across the street toward them. "Hi, Jenna," she said cheerily, but her voice held an undercurrent of suppressed excitement.

Harvey noticed too. "What's going on?" he asked.

"It's that Los Angeles woman."

"Barbara Raymond?" Jenna asked.

"Yes, Mrs. Raymond. She's dead."

Harvey dropped a can of paint into the trunk with a jarring thud. "Dead," he repeated.

Megan could barely contain her eagerness. "They found her body on the rocks below the pier."

"Drowned?" he asked.

"No." She leaned in to whisper conspiratorially, "They think she was murdered."

Harvey and Jenna stared at her, speechless. Jenna remembered the two men searching below her in the morning—for evidence of a crime, for a body?—and the police car passing the house. Barbara Raymond was a beautiful, vibrant woman—how could she be dead? Worse, murdered. Who would want her dead? Who, in this quiet, out-of-the-way small town, where big-city crime was presumed not to intrude, would take the life of an elegant yet friendly stranger? "She's too beautiful," Rick had said. "Women like that are nothing but trouble." Perhaps she had brought the trouble with her, or it had followed her from L.A. A stranger would stand out in this place, but who knew what might creep in while they were all peacefully asleep in their safe, quiet houses? Scary.

There was a moment of awkwardness before she realized they were waiting for her to leave before continuing the conversation. "Thanks, Harvey," she said. "I'll let you know about ordering more paint." She slid into the front seat and pulled out from the curb. Harvey and Megan stood in the middle of the street and watched her go.

As she drove in, she noticed two cars in the driveway next door, but nobody outside. In her own driveway, she sat for a moment, overwhelmed by a new, sharp feeling of dread. San Ignacio, once a peaceful refuge, had in the space of a few seconds, in the words of a pretty young woman, become dangerous, sinister. She stepped out of the car and felt small, insignificant, as if she might be swallowed up by the enormous sky. What was the opposite of claustrophobia? Agoraphobia?

She had intended to put the paint in the shed, but now she was reluctant to go into the dusty darkness and left the cans in the car. The front door was unlocked—a natural choice only an hour ago. She had not supposed anybody, even the mischievous Nancy, would enter uninvited. Where had she put the small brass key?

She closed the door behind her and stood still in the nearly bare living room. A rush of fear and loneliness brought a lump to her throat. She walked slowly into the bedroom, and her gaze went straight to the portrait of her grandmother above the bed. It was a good likeness, with enough life in the eyes to suggest she was about to speak. Jenna drew closer and touched the glass as she would have touched her grandmother's cheek, and without warning she wept—not for Gran, but for Patrick. No, not even for Patrick—to hell with him!—for her lost love, the love he had betrayed.

She felt better afterward, calmer, but still unsettled. Fortunately, she had blown her nose and washed her face by the time Nancy came to tell her what she already knew.

"*Murdered*," Nancy said with great relish. "Just like on TV."

"But *not* like on TV," Jenna said gently. "A real person, a person we knew, at least a little. Not an actress who can go on to another part. A real woman, really dead. Her family and friends will be terribly sad."

"Did she have a family?" Nancy asked, as if she would know, and more urgently, "Do you think she went to heaven?"

"I hope so." She wasn't going to get into a religious discussion with someone else's child. She was trying not to remember Barbara Raymond at all. She was a stranger—not only to her, but to everyone in town. They had exchanged only a few words—less than Jenna had shared in casual conversations with store clerks and taxi drivers—and except for her exceptional beauty, Mrs. Raymond might have left no impression at all. The news of her death should be no more personal than crime statistics in the newspaper. Yet—here and now—it was.

After Nancy had gone home, she disciplined herself to get some work done on the book. The need to concentrate, the precision required, even the boredom of repetition calmed her. Only when darkness fell did unease creep back in.

She found the old-fashioned brass key where she had dropped it in a kitchen drawer and locked the front door. She had nothing she could use as a weapon, and sleeping with a kitchen knife would have been ridiculous. She lay awake for a long time, listening for suspicious sounds, mistrusting every creak in the old house. When she slept it was restlessly, with jumbled, incoherent dreams.

Chapter Five

Monday, February 18 (Washington's Birthday):
Air Force helicopter search team rescues U.S. pilot
who parachuted from disabled plane 40 miles north of
Saudi border.

In the morning, of course, Jenna's fears seemed
very foolish. Mrs. Raymond was not from San Ignacio.
She did not belong here. The roots of this tragedy were
in her, not in this place. She had told Nancy it was not
like TV, so what was the reality? She had yet to hear
any details that would suggest a likely scenario.
Ockham's razor—the simplest solution was the best.

Very well. Barbara Raymond was not murdered. It
was only gossip. Megan Wells had said she was
murdered—but what did she know? Nancy had said the
same thing about Rick Alvarez's wife, and Rosalie had
said nobody knew anything of the sort. She couldn't
depend on gossip and rumors. She should get a TV or
subscribe to a newspaper—was there a local paper? If
only she could get the local news without inviting the
Gulf War in.

Megan had said "they think" she was murdered.
San Ignacio didn't have the resources of a large city
police department. They might be mistaken. Mrs.
Raymond fell and hit her head. She took a midnight
swim and drowned. When had she last been seen—at

the barbecue? Was she involved in a messy divorce? A custody dispute? Did she have a jealous lover? Was she, as Rick had said, "too beautiful" and "nothing but trouble"?

Jenna had no answers, and indeed she needed none. She was not an amateur detective in a cozy whodunit. Her story was about something else entirely—although she had to admit she wasn't sure exactly what it was. Her grandfather had left her this house, and she was going to live here, make a life for herself.

After breakfast, she took the paint cans out of the car and put them in the shed. Nothing lurked in the shadows. She found an old brush and took the top off one can. She wasn't ready to paint yet, but she wanted to see how it would look.

She chose a partially shaded area on the side of the house and painted a two-foot square patch. She stepped back and eyed the result critically. Not bad. She had intended to paint the whole house herself, even if she had to do it a little at a time, but now, taking in the peeling paint around the windows, near the ground, and up under the eaves, she reconsidered.

She wanted the job done properly, with thorough preparation. She didn't much want to climb a ladder, if she even had one in the shed. She didn't want anybody to criticize her sloppy brushwork. Nor did she want the help of teenage amateurs, even if Harvey vouched for them. They would probably make a mess, and she would be liable if they fell off a ladder. No, she wanted a fast, careful, efficient, professional job—even if it meant having Rick Alvarez underfoot for a few more days. At least she knew he had a ladder.

On the other hand, she did not want to walk or

drive down the road and ask him to do it. It was ridiculously inconvenient that he didn't have a phone. Why didn't he? It was absurd, at the end of the twentieth century, especially for a man who did freelance work for his neighbors. She remembered that Gabe Burrows had seemed hostile to him—because he wouldn't have a phone put in? Or had Rick refused to have one put in because of Gabe's hostility or whatever had provoked it? The question was moot, because she didn't want to call him, either.

She was back inside, writing a letter to her parents, when Rosalie Hayes ambled over to return the cracker tin Jenna had used for the cookies. In true small-town friendly fashion, Rosalie had filled the tin with freshly baked cream cheese brownies. Jenna made coffee, and they sat at the kitchen table, munching sweet, moist brownies and talking. Topic number one, of course, was the murder of Barbara Raymond.

No, her death wasn't an accident. She didn't drown or hit her head. She was stabbed several times with a thin blade, like a small fishing knife, the kind half of San Ignacio used every day. This information was apparently reliable—it had come straight from the local police chief, Vince Allan. No suspects had been named, which meant everyone was a suspect. Chief Allan had no personal information about Mrs. Raymond, except that she was a widow and had no children. So no nasty divorce or custody case. Her husband had died six years ago. By the look of her, she might have had any number of jealous lovers or would-be lovers.

When the juiciest subjects had been exhausted, Rosalie remembered she had laundry to do, and Jenna, even though she could make her own hours, did have a deadline. "I'll let you go," Rosalie said, an expression Jenna hadn't heard since her grandmother's time.

She had passed the point where she could get any work done at the kitchen table and tried setting up a work station in the guest bedroom. The space wasn't ideal, but the light was good, and the drafting table wouldn't be in the way as it would in the living room. She worked steadily with T-square and pencils until her stomach told her she needed something more nutritious than Rosalie's cream cheese brownies. It was past lunchtime.

She opted for the fastest protein lunch available—a peanut butter sandwich—and sat down to finish her letter. She had written about the Hayes family and the barbecue, about having the roof fixed, and her progress on the book. Nothing to suggest discouragement or uncertainty, nothing about the murder. Now she described the brownies, praised Rosalie's neighborliness, and rhapsodized about the ocean view. She wondered if she was fooling anybody, herself included.

Tires crunched on gravel, and this time she recognized the sound. Rick Alvarez was back. "Another interruption," she wrote. "For such a small, out-of-the-way place, we seem to have a very brisk social life." She left the letter on the table but took her sandwich with her to the front door to let him know he had interrupted her again.

He got out of the pickup with a rolled paper in one hand and strode toward the house. He wasn't wearing his tool belt. Jenna opened the door and stepped out on the porch. Again she waited for him to speak first.

"Hi," he said. He seemed as supremely confident

as ever, but stopped at the foot of the steps because she hadn't responded.

"Hello," she said finally, and automatically, "Where's Danny?"

"With a friend," he said. "I have an hour." He came on up the steps. "I brought you something." He held up the rolled paper but didn't offer it to her. She would have to invite him inside. She took a bite out of her sandwich and gestured for him to enter. He followed her into the kitchen, where the letter lay on the table with the pen across it, clearly unfinished. Rosalie had apologized for her timing. Rick didn't notice. Rosalie had offered information and delicious brownies. What had he brought?

He spread the paper out on the other side of the table, revealing a drawing of a kitchen. Not blueprints, not an artistic rendering, but a sketch done with an ordinary pencil and ruler. It was nevertheless a thing of beauty. It suggested, without the niceties of shading and perspective she was used to, an efficiently organized and attractively arranged kitchen, a reimagining of the space she stood in. He had given her a walk-in pantry as well as a shelf for a microwave. "The window is here," he said, as if she couldn't see for herself. She was so annoyed with him, and he had created this for her, and damn it, the thing was perfect.

"If you like Rosalie's cabinets," he began, and Jenna put up a hand to hold him off.

"We don't need to get into the details," she said. "I probably can't afford it anyway, and I have work to do."

"Okay," he said, and she couldn't tell if he was surprised or offended. He started to roll the plan up again, and she reached out to stop him. Without meaning to, she closed her hand on his. She let go at once and felt her face go hot.

"Leave it," she said. "I'd like to think about it."

"Okay," he said again. "You can let me know." He glanced around the kitchen, and his gaze fell on the letter lying on the table. She both did and did not want him to see the drafting table instead and know she had been seriously working. Why did she care?

She could let him know, he said, but she couldn't call him. "Why," she began—and stopped. She was being rude and wanted to be ruder. Instead she took a deep breath. "I appreciate what you did," she said, gesturing at the plan. "I can't do it right now, but—I can see you worked hard on it."

"No problem," he said. He sounded like he meant it. She knew it would be awkward to ask him to do the painting now, but she couldn't face a retreat to her previous position of self-reliance. "I want to get the exterior painted first," she said. "If you'd be interested…"

"I don't do a lot of painting," he said, "but…sure. I'll give you a discount."

"Why?" she asked bluntly. A better question was why she wanted to question his motives.

"You're Bill Scott's granddaughter."

"Yes. And…?" He couldn't have known her grandfather very well, having lived here for only three years.

"I kind of owe him," he said. "Anyway, I can paint the house for you. It'll take a few days, but I can start…probably Thursday."

"*Probably* Thursday," Jenna repeated. "I know you

can't call first, but it would be better if I knew when to expect you."

"Sorry," he said. He didn't sound very sorry, but neither did he have the tone, so familiar to her from her life with Patrick, that suggested she was the one with the problem. "Let's say Thursday at eight, unless it rains."

"It must be inconvenient not having a phone," she said.

He shrugged. "It can be, but it's a small town. People talk to each other face to face. They walk. There are kids with bicycles who can carry messages."

"Do you tip them?" she asked.

"Who?"

"The kids with bicycles."

He shook his head, not in negation, but in amazement. "What are you being so prickly about?" he asked.

The phone rang. "Excuse me," she said and picked up the receiver. It was her first call.

"Having one can be inconvenient too," he said

A bit flustered, Jenna answered the phone. It was Harvey Wells. He had ordered her paint, but the green wasn't immediately available. Did she want to wait or make another choice? She couldn't quite focus on the problem. "Rick Alvarez is here," she said. "He's going to do the painting. Maybe you should talk to him." She held out the receiver. "Harvey Wells," she said.

He took the phone and quickly determined the trim paint would be available by the time he was ready for it. He didn't sound like a man with a phobia about phones. He asked after Megan, which Jenna hadn't thought to do, and confirmed a date to play poker. Taking his sweet time standing in her kitchen, when she'd told him she had work to do. He might have read her mind, because he looked right at her and said conversationally, "I don't think she likes me." Whatever Harvey said in response made him smile. "Yeah, okay, Harvey. I'll see you later." He hung up, and before she could think of anything to break an awkward silence, he said, "I'll get out of your hair," and started to leave.

"Wait," she said. "Rosalie made brownies. Would you—?" He shook his head before she could finish. "I remember—you don't like chocolate. But Danny—?"

"Thank you," he said. "He would like that." He waited while she wrapped three brownies in aluminum foil. "Thank you," he said again. "I'll see you Thursday."

He started out the door, stopped, and turned back. "What do you call that color?" he asked.

"What?" She stared at him, her mind going logically to paint, but he lifted a hand and took a lock of her hair between his fingers. She could barely feel the contact, but it made her heart beat a little faster. "Oh," she said, trying not to sound flustered. "Auburn, I guess."

"Auburn," he repeated, and then he was gone, leaving her standing in her kitchen, completely incapable of thinking about work.

"What?" she said again. What was it with this guy? After a few very confused seconds, she reminded herself he was an artist. Ah, yes, aesthetic curiosity, nothing more.

She did manage to get a decent amount of work done in the afternoon and finished her letter. She studied Rick's sketch—he had labeled it *Scott Kitchen*—and tacked it up next to the sink. She reminded herself she had priorities to consider and went outside to study the paint square again. She stepped back and tried to visualize the forest-green trim. Only then did she remember she had forgotten to ask him for an estimate, with or without the discount.

Footsteps sounded behind her, a familiar, light tread. "Hi, Nancy," she said without turning around.

"Hi, Miss Scott." The girl came to stand beside her and study the test patch. "White is boring," she pronounced.

"No, it isn't. It's clean and fresh. I like it." Fresh was what she needed—a fresh start.

"But it's still boring."

"Sorry," she said. "What have you been up to?"

"School. Also boring. I hate fractions, don't you?"

"Not my favorite thing," Jenna agreed. "What have you been reading?"

"I finished the one about whales. It was good. Now I'm reading the one about stars—but it isn't, really."

"That's as clear as mud," Jenna said with a smile.

"It's about a girl in Denmark," Nancy explained. "The title is something about stars. The Nazis were very bad. Are they all dead?"

"Yes, all dead, before you were born, even before I was born."

"Good. I dreamed about them last night."

"That must have been scary."

"Yes," Nancy agreed, "but I was brave. Are you brave?"

"Not very. I guess I could be if I had to."

"Me too. Who do you think killed Mrs.

Raymond?"

"I don't know. Whoever he is, I hope he's gone." She also hoped she wasn't encouraging ideas Rosalie and Mike would prefer to dismiss. Being admired by other people's children carried a certain responsibility. Which reminded her…

"Is Larry still mad at me?" she asked.

"I don't know," Nancy said disinterestedly. "He's sure mad at somebody. But all he cares about is the stupid war and stupid Heather."

"Heather seems like a nice girl," Jenna objected.

"Yeah, but *stupid*, hanging around with my dumb brother. I think love makes people stupid."

"You may be right." Yes, love had made her stupid. She was through with love, thank God. The tears she had shed for Patrick yesterday seemed remote and foolish. She was better off without him, better off without romantic entanglements of any kind, admiring teenage boys included.

When Nancy had gone next door to do her homework, Jenna did more work on the illustrations, enough to let her count the day as a success.

She slept well, without nightmares of murder, Nazis, or even deadlines.

Chapter Six

Thursday, February 21: Defense Secretary Dick Cheney says allies are preparing "one of the largest land assaults of modern times."

It didn't rain on Thursday, and Rick Alvarez showed up exactly on time, at eight o'clock. Jenna had gotten up early, just in case, and was washing the breakfast dishes when he drove in. He didn't come to the door, and she didn't go out to greet him. She was unsure of what their relationship should be—he was a contractor, doing work for her for pay, but he was also a small-town neighbor and Danny's father. He thought she didn't like him—or had he only been joking with Harvey?

When she finished the dishes, she looked through the front window. He had spread drop cloths and removed the damaged boards on the steps. Annoyed, she started toward the door to tell him what she thought of his presumption. He hadn't even given her an estimate for the painting before he started adding things to the bill. He had to make a living, but she couldn't afford to support him and Danny as well as herself.

With her hand on the doorknob, she stopped long enough to reconsider. She didn't want to make a fool of herself—if she hadn't already done so. She considered the situation from his point of view. He had known and admired her grandfather and believed he owed him something. He probably knew this house well and could judge its requirements better than she could. He was a professional, even though he hadn't been doing it very long, seemed competent, and apparently liked his work. He might be used to having a free hand and expecting her to trust him to give her what she needed. *Everything she asked for*, she remembered Jim Kelly saying. *Couldn't say about what she needs*. She blushed and let go of the doorknob.

Rick laid a new board across the first step and started noisily banging in nails. She could no longer pretend she didn't know he was here. She took a deep breath and opened the door. "Good morning," she said.

He stopped hammering. "Good morning." He seemed as wary as she was. "There's no point in painting damaged wood," he explained. "The porch is fine—it was just these two steps."

Jenna said nothing. When had he measured the steps? Before or after she had asked him to paint? She supposed he would rather she hadn't come out. He knew what he was doing, and she should leave him to it. She wanted to be neighborly, but couldn't think of a single thing to say. The one question she should ask—how much this was going to cost—now seemed embarrassingly awkward. "Okay," she said finally, "I'll get out of your hair," and then remembered he had said the same thing to her the last time they met and might think she was mocking him. Right after he had said it, he had asked about the color of her hair, and *his* hair—thick, black, curling a little at the back of his neck as he bent to drive in another nail…

Oh, my God. I am losing it. She retreated into the

house. She resolved to ignore his very existence unless he came to the door with a question. She put away the dishes and went into the guest bedroom to work on a cutaway drawing. She struggled to concentrate and only partly succeeded. She heard—or imagined—sounds outside. The ladder banging against the house? The scraping of paint? A whirring—perhaps a sander? A whistling sound—yes, he was whistling. He did enjoy his work. Why else would he do it? He was definitely overqualified. What was the tune he was whistling? *Concentrate, Jenna, concentrate.*

She expected him to stop at noon to eat lunch in the pickup, as he had when he was repairing the roof, but instead he drove away before twelve. She didn't see which way he headed—home for lunch, to town for supplies? No matter. She breathed more easily when he was gone. Why was it so oppressive just to have someone working on her property?

He was gone about an hour and got right back to work. To prove to herself she wasn't a total coward, she went out to check on his progress. He had obviously been doing a very thorough, careful preparation. She could see places where he had sanded, spackled, and replaced caulking. The window screens he had removed were carefully stacked.

"How's it going?" she asked, trying to sound casual and not as if she meant *How much longer is this going to take?*

"Fine," he said. "I'll start painting tomorrow."

"Are you going to use a sprayer?" she asked.

He shook his head. "A roller."

She couldn't think of anything else to ask, so she tried the one subject that made him seem most human.

"When do you have to pick Danny up?"

"Whenever I'm finished here," he said. "He's going to a friend's after school—Connor O'Hara? He was at the barbecue."

She nodded, although she didn't remember which one Connor was. "Okay, I'll leave you to it," she said and retreated to the guest room and her drafting table.

She was concentrating on her work and didn't know how much time had passed when the screen door banged. She heard Rick's footsteps—those boots, such a masculine sound—and he called out, "Jenna?…Miss Scott?"

She met him in the hall and countered with, "Mr. Alvarez?"

"Sorry—Jenna. I knocked…"

"I was in the bedroom."

"I just wanted to tell you I'm done for today and I'll come back tomorrow at eight. Mind if I—?" He gestured toward the kitchen with both hands palm up so she could see how dirty they were.

"Oh, yes, of course." He paced ahead of her into the kitchen and washed his hands at the sink.

"You're going to get Danny now?" she asked.

"Yes. He loved the brownies, by the way."

"Would you like a few more?"

"No, no, three was enough. Thank you." He held up his dripping hands, and she offered him a dish towel. While he used it, his gaze fell on the sketch she had tacked up beside the sink. Again she had the odd feeling that she knew what he was thinking, which was absurd, when he had never given her any clues about anything. But she knew he had worked hard on this plan and wanted to make it a reality, and she was both the means to that end and a major obstacle.

He stepped toward her to hand back the dish towel, but he was too close for comfort. She had her back to the table and couldn't go far. It was amazing how quickly he could rile her. "Does the concept of personal space mean anything to you?" she asked.

"Sorry," he said, but he didn't sound sorry, and he didn't back away. Instead, he put his hand on her arm and leaned in to kiss her. *Whoa!* Out of context, the kiss was a good one, but it was of course perfectly outrageous. She pushed him away. She wanted very badly to slap his face—did women actually do that, or was it too melodramatic? What if he hit her back? Her heart was pounding. "I'm sorry," he said, and this time the apology sounded more genuine. "I couldn't resist."

"Try harder!" she snapped. She could see he liked that—oh, yes, no doubt her outrage was very amusing to him. "Who raised you?" she demanded.

He put up his hands in a gesture of surrender, said, "Sorry" again, and left the room. She waited, almost holding her breath, until he left the house, letting the screen door bang behind him, and then she followed.

He was putting his equipment in the pickup, and she stood on the porch to watch him go. She hoped he would be embarrassed, reminded that this was her property and he was working here. He could be in real trouble. She could file a complaint against his contractor's license, assuming he even had one. In the city she could have made one phone call, and if he wasn't promptly fired at least he would never be in her house again.

She saw Nancy Hayes running down the hill from next door, coming over after school as she had before, and she went down the steps to meet her. Nancy waved, but when she saw Rick getting into his pickup she stopped dead in her tracks. She looked frightened. Hadn't she said she thought Danny's father was nice? What was she afraid of?

Rick drove away without a backward glance, and Nancy approached the house without her usual bounce. "Hi," Jenna said. "What's wrong?" Even if the girl could feel her anger, she shouldn't be so frightened.

She came right up to the steps before she spoke. "He killed Mrs. Raymond," she said.

"Who?"

"*Him*. Danny's father."

"No, of course he didn't," Jenna said at once. "Why would you say such a thing?"

"Everybody says so." Her certainty carried a chilling persuasiveness.

But no, it wasn't true. "Remember what your mom said about gossip."

"It isn't gossip if it's true," Nancy said sulkily. It was a familiar refrain.

"Who said it was?"

"Everybody," Nancy insisted.

"Kids at school?"

"Everybody," she repeated. "It's true. He killed Danny's mother, too."

"Nancy!" Jenna spoke so sharply that the girl jumped.

"He—"

"Don't say it! Don't say another word." She was furious, horrified.

Nancy turned around and ran home.

It wasn't true. It *wasn't* true. He was Danny's

76

father. She had seen the sweetness between them. Five minutes ago he had kissed her. It was wrong and, God help her, she had liked it. She could still feel the gentle intensity of his lips against hers. He might be presumptuous, exasperating, and too damned attractive for his own good, but he wasn't a killer.

Oh, God—Danny. If Nancy had heard this at school, what about Danny? Would the other kids have told Danny this ugly lie?

She didn't get any work done for the rest of the day.

She locked the door before she went to bed.

Chapter Seven

Friday, February 22: President Bush demands Iraq begin withdrawal from Kuwait by noon February 23 to avoid ground war.

In the morning, Jenna's very first waking thought, as she surfaced out of a dream, was—I am not going to get this damned house painted. As disturbing as Nancy's words had been, she had sternly dismissed them. The kiss was another matter. She needed to talk to somebody else about this; she needed some advice. Rosalie Hayes was her first choice. Did he have a reputation around San Ignacio that would put her own in question if she continued to work with him? The Latin lover—a stereotype, worse than a stereotype, really a cliché, a *silly* cliché. Rosalie liked him, and he had made her those beautiful cabinets. Monica had been friendly with him. They were both married women— was that possible? Was this San Ignacio or Peyton Place? Did he think—and this made the hairs on the back of her neck stand up—this was the kind of discount he was giving her?

Then again, maybe a kiss was just a kiss. Against her will, which was legally assault, but her resistance had been minimal. He had apologized—and he had put them both in an extremely awkward position. She couldn't see how they could even face each other again.

While she ate breakfast she decided she would go next door first thing and ask, as discreetly as possible, if there was anything she should worry about. She hoped Rosalie's disapproval had kept Nancy from telling her about the gossip. Ought she to call first or just walk up the hill?

Tires crunched on gravel. *Damn!* Now she would have to deal with him first—and walk up the hill with his eyes on her? She got up and put the dishes in the sink. What if he came to the door? This was intolerable; she could not be afraid in her own house. She picked up her purse and the cardboard box Jim Kelly had given her. She did need groceries, and she could stop at Rosalie's before she drove into town.

Rick was carrying cans of paint from the pickup when she came out. He wore paint-spattered white pants and shirt instead of his usual jeans. She strode purposefully toward her car without looking in his direction. The morning was beautiful, clear and sunny, with all the promise of California's early spring.

"Jenna," he said urgently. He put down the cans of paint and approached her, and she stopped and waited, chin up.

"Good morning," she said coolly.

"Morning," he echoed. "Listen, I'm sorry if I was out of line yesterday."

"If?" she said. He sounded sincere, but she hated that he was so calm. He was always so self-assured. Had he thought of the danger to his license? "Were you trying to collect for the discount?" she asked.

"No!" he said. Ah, she had gotten under his skin that time. "God—no. I just wanted to kiss you. It was inappropriate, and it won't happen again. I'm really sorry."

"Okay," she said. "Apology accepted," and she strode on to her car. Knowing how well she had handled herself gave her a thrill of satisfaction. She hadn't become flustered or made a fool of herself. *Good job, Jenna.* She resisted checking in the rearview mirror to see if he was still standing there or had started work. Rosalie's car wasn't in the driveway, so she drove on to town.

As soon as she walked into Sam's Grocery she knew Nancy hadn't made anything up. Gathered inside were Rosalie, Gabe Burrows, Jim Kelly of course, and three other people she either hadn't met or didn't remember—a thin brunette and an older couple with matching glasses and white hair. They all looked in her direction, and their expressions, excited and a little guilty, told her they had been gossiping. She could easily guess what the subject was.

They had no facts, of course. Chief Allan had no evidence, no suspects. He had posted a notice in the store asking anyone with information, anyone who might have been the last to see Barbara Raymond alive, to contact him. The body had been sent to Carroll City, where they had a coroner and a crime lab.

Rick Alvarez had been tried and convicted in the court of public opinion. Apparently he didn't know. She hoped Danny didn't know. Everybody else, it seemed, had heard the rumors.

"This is awful," she said. "Who started this? He's at my house right now, painting." She realized she could easily fan the fire by telling them he had forced himself on her, but a derisive voice in her head said, *Lighten up, lady; it was only a kiss.*

"You shouldn't leave him alone in your house," Gabe Burrows said.

"Don't, Gabe," Rosalie said. She had apparently heard this before. "Rick is no thief, and I don't believe he's a killer, either." She didn't, but she relished the juiciness of the gossip. Jenna had seen signs the very first day in her kitchen that she liked to gossip, even though she deplored the habit in Nancy. Like mother, like daughter. Jenna was sickened—and now she couldn't possibly ask her if he was a sexual predator.

"You're too trusting," Gabe told Rosalie. "You take everybody at face value."

The thin, dark-haired woman stepped forward and offered Jenna her hand. "We haven't met," she said, "I'm Charlene Dickens."

"Jenna Scott," she replied, but she didn't take Charlene's hand. "I understood the police didn't have any suspects. Why do you think Rick Alvarez did it?"

There was an eager rush to fill her in on all the supposed details. Some of them gave her pause, but others were completely ridiculous. He, or at least his pickup, had been seen at Mrs. Raymond's cabin. He hadn't been in church the morning after. He owned a knife. They were both from L.A.

"It's a big place," Jenna pointed out, trying to be the voice of reason. More than three million people lived in Los Angeles! "Where was Danny when Rick was with Barbara Raymond?" she asked.

"You can scoff," Charlene said, "but don't be surprised when Vince shows up to arrest him."

"A man who would murder one woman wouldn't hesitate at a second," the older lady said. "He killed his own wife."

"There have been rumors since he first came," Rosalie said, "but nobody really knows—where's the proof?"

"Oh, I know he did it," Charlene said. "It was in the newspapers. I was working in the city at the time, and I remember—"

"Yesterday you said you weren't sure," Rosalie countered.

"Well, I remember now. Don't you think it's suspicious that he never talks about her? Not a single word to anybody about the boy's mother? What do you suppose he's hiding if he didn't kill her? And he doesn't wear a wedding ring," she added triumphantly.

"If it was in the papers," Jenna asked, "why is he walking around free?"

"Oh, he got off on a technicality or something. It happens all the time. Now he's here, and he's done it again, and none of us is safe." She folded her arms and smiled smugly.

Jenna wanted to slap her. "Did you start these rumors?" she asked.

"They're not rumors," Charlene said, "and I didn't start anything; I heard it from several people. I'm not making things up."

"I don't believe any of this," Jenna said.

"I don't either," said Rosalie. "Not that he murdered his wife, or that he would have deliberately killed Mrs. Raymond. Maybe some kind of accident…"

"She was stabbed several times," the older man said. "He would have been hard put to do that accidentally."

Jenna turned to Jim Kelly, who hadn't said a word since she entered. "I came in to get groceries," she said.

She couldn't tell how he felt about the gossip, but he helped her gather what she needed.

"Do you want me to go home with you?" Rosalie asked.

"No. I'm not afraid of Rick Alvarez!" At least not that way.

"Do you buy any of this?" she asked Jim Kelly as he put the box in the trunk.

"It's a small town," he said noncommittally. "People talk." His store was the hub of the community; perhaps he was wise not to take sides.

"Thank you," she said, and he went back into the store. If there were sides to be taken here, she would choose the side of Rick and Danny. She banged the trunk lid down, left the car there, and marched across the street to the hardware store.

Harvey wasn't in, but Megan was, sitting prettily behind the counter reading a paperback book. "Oh, hi," she said, giving Jenna an oddly guilty look. Had she been scandal-mongering too?

"Good morning," Jenna said coolly.

"Everything okay with the paint?" Megan asked. They had sold her the paint and arranged with Rick for its delivery. Harvey played cards with him. These were not strangers; they were neighbors. They had known him for three years and, although they barely knew her, they had known her grandfather. This was not like reading the *National Enquirer*. Real people were involved—beautiful, ill-fated Barbara Raymond, skilled handyman Rick Alvarez, sweet-natured little Danny.

Jenna walked over to the Local Artists case and picked up the little carving of the sleeping cat. A foolish gesture maybe, but the wood had a cool, comforting feeling in her hand. She paid Megan without saying another word and stalked out.

Doubts crept in as she drove home. It sounded like such nonsense, but could it be all smoke and no fire? What if Rick had tried to kiss Mrs. Raymond—"I couldn't resist"—and she had fought back, slapped his face? The little carving in her pocket was proof of his skill with a knife. Oh, please, she thought, Danny's already lost his mother. Let's not railroad his father. She had considered locking the front door when she left, but hadn't. She didn't know whether she should regret the lapse now or not.

When she drove in, he was nowhere in sight. The sun was shining on the front of the house, and it was better not to paint in direct sunlight, so he might be around back. Or he might be inside waiting for her. Against her rational will, the hairs on the back of her neck stood up. This was the scene in the movie where the audience would yell, "Don't go in the house!"

She took the box of groceries and went slowly inside. She listened for any suspicious sound and didn't hear anything, but when she passed the guest bedroom, Rick was standing inside the doorway. Would his audacity never end? Anger trumped fear. She slammed the box down on the kitchen table and marched in to give him a piece of her mind.

He was staring at the nearly-finished cutaway on her drafting table. He looked up as she approached and said, "Wow!" He gave her a look of astonished respect. "Is this what you've been working on?" he asked.

"Yes, but—"

"What's it for?"

She took a deep breath to calm herself. "A book—

about alternate energy sources," she said. "What—"

"Wow," he said again. He shook his head in genuine appreciation. "You don't use a computer?"

"CAD? No, I'll probably have to eventually. They're taking over. Why—?"

"I'd better get back to work," he said, and then he simply left the house, giving her no clue as to why he had been inside in the first place. Every time she thought she knew where she was with him, he threw her another curve.

She knew she should tell him about the rumors before he heard worse somewhere else—would any of these gossiping cowards say those things to his face? She should tell him, if only so he could protect Danny. Kids could be cruel. Even here someone might taunt Danny. These were good people, churchgoing families, and yet they were so quick to believe the worst and spread lies.

Be fair, she thought. She had only talked to a few people. Nancy's "everybody" might be a few idiots with time on their hands. Maybe she shouldn't dignify this nonsense by repeating it to Rick.

No, she should. She definitely should.

She didn't.

She put the little carving of the sleeping cat on her bedside table, a small symbol of defiance. It was also very beautiful. Would a man who created such beauty with a knife use the same tool to end a woman's life?

Rick certainly seemed unaware of any of this drama behind the scenes. He must know about the murder, but he had never even mentioned it to her in passing. He worked all morning painting her house, doing a neat, careful job. He left again at lunchtime and drove back sooner than she expected.

She was still trying to figure out what to do about the gossip. Small town, small minds. Would they do more than talk—boycott his business, burn down his house, steal his tools? He should be warned. Maybe somebody else—Rosalie? Harvey?—would tell him. Maybe it would all die down. Or maybe she would become a target herself because she was harboring a murderer…or at least giving him a job.

Rick, oblivious to rumors, with an apparently clear conscience, whistled while he worked. She looked out to see what he was doing, and *oh, my God*, he was taking off his shirt! In February? Oh, all right, the day was warm, and he was working hard. He was broad-shouldered, well-muscled, a shade browner than her best summer tan, with only a little wiry black chest hair. *¡Ay, caramba!* Maybe she would pray for rain.

At the end of the day, he knocked on the door—this time she heard him—to ask if she wanted him to continue the next day. He was wearing his shirt.

"I'll have to bring Danny because it's Saturday. It's up to you—it works for me either way. I can come back on Monday instead."

"Won't it be boring for Danny?" she asked.

He shook his head. "He can help," he said and, maybe in case she objected to child labor, quickly added, "or play or read."

Jenna hesitated. She would love two days respite from this constant distraction and tension. She would also like to get it done with as soon as possible, and surely Rick wouldn't try anything with Danny around. In the end, the decision was more about the feeling that Danny, if not Rick, was safer here, painting her house, than out in the dangerous, gossiping world. "Fine," she said. "Come tomorrow. Bring Danny. If you like, I'll make you both lunch."

"That would be great," he said. "I'll see you tomorrow. Oh—nine o'clock?"

"Fine," she said again. That was that—no awkwardness. Apology made and accepted. He had been a perfect gentleman. No doubt she was an idiot.

****

Only when she awoke in the middle of the night, in the too-quiet darkness, did the doubts creep in again. Things always seemed worst in the middle of the night, she reminded herself, but fear took hold, and a particular horror on Danny's behalf.

Rick had never shown the slightest sign of guilt. He hadn't been nervous or upset when she had seen him soon after the murder—but he never was. Sunday morning, when they had sat casually on the steps, and he had told her he was a teacher in L.A.—that was not the demeanor of a troubled conscience. But when the police car zoomed by, everything changed. She had been sure she knew the reason, but wasn't that romantic nonsense? Maybe the fear evoked by the sight of the car was not for the possibility of danger to Danny but for his own discovery? If he wasn't the killer, who was? If it was a stranger, someone from out of town, might he still be out there in the dark? What was the creaking sound she was hearing? No, it was only the old house settling.

What the hell was Rick up to in the house while she was gone? She wasn't sure whether the drafting table was visible without stepping inside, whether he could have spotted it as he passed by. She would have to check. Maybe she had left the guest bedroom window open, and he needed to close it before painting?

A dog barked somewhere in the distance. Had she remembered to lock the front door?

Why hadn't he said anything to anybody in San Ignacio about his late wife—in three years, not one word? Was his silence merely the exaggeration of a silly gossip? Had anybody asked? A lot of married men didn't wear wedding rings in any case, and it might be inconvenient when working with tools. He was no longer married. It was ludicrous to suppose it had any significance.

Did Rosalie's belief Rick could have killed Mrs. Raymond by accident mean she knew or suspected he was likely to have approached her, because he had a history of sleeping around? *I couldn't resist...I just wanted to kiss you.*

What had he said about Barbara Raymond at the barbecue? She remembered precisely and didn't want to remember. Where had he been during the hour or so when she didn't see him, and why did he leave so early? Because Danny was tired. He did own a knife, of course, but almost every man in San Ignacio did. Why would he murder a woman he didn't even know? How could anyone know whether he had known her before or not? They were both from L.A.

Why had he left L.A. and teaching? Had he left voluntarily, or was he fired or asked to leave because of a scandal? Why would he have killed his wife? Not money—anger, jealousy, a custody dispute? Or what if she had been terminally ill and it was a mercy killing? But surely not with a knife...

Why didn't Rick want Danny to speak Spanish? Oh, now she *was* being ridiculous.

Who started the gossip? Why were so many people so quick to believe in his guilt? Because he was a relative outsider, a latecomer? She didn't think they were racist, but she didn't know what her own feelings about him were. What did she know about him? Good father, good craftsman…good kisser. Hadn't she read a murder mystery in which the handyman did it?

If she was ever going to get back to sleep, she must trust that these shadows would vanish in the morning light.

Chapter Eight

Saturday, February 23: Allies' ground offensive begins at 5 p.m. PST.

Saturday was easier. Danny lightened the mood considerably. Rick had dressed him in old clothes and let him get paint all over himself as long as he stayed on the drop cloths. She hadn't wanted amateur help, but trusted Rick to correct Danny's mistakes. Yes, he seemed trustworthy, not someone you would suspect of murder. Nancy, so often underfoot before, was conspicuous by her absence, but Jenna didn't suppose he would notice.

She had been afraid having to keep an eye on Danny would slow him down, but the work was going very quickly. She could hear their voices from time to time, and once she heard Danny trying to whistle. She hoped he would stay off the ladder. He was such a great kid. What would happen to him if his father was charged with murder? Did he have grandparents somewhere?

She didn't want to suggest Rick was no longer welcome in her kitchen, although in fact he wasn't, but she served lunch on the porch, and the three of them sat together and ate tuna sandwiches, apples, potato chips, and the last three of Rosalie's brownies. Danny ate two of the brownies and most of the potato chips and did almost all the talking, his usual shyness swamped by the joy of creative labor. Like father, like son.

Unlike Nancy, he liked school. He liked everything about it. Reading, arithmetic, art, recess, everything. Today at least, he wanted to be a painter when he grew up, but she was sure being a truck driver was a more usual ambition. "Your house is very easy to paint," he told Jenna. "It's only a little house." There was paint on his face, and he had added a milk mustache, so he resembled an impish little clown.

"How is your house?" she asked. "Is it sad today?"

"No, it's happy," he said blithely. Rick raised an eyebrow, but said nothing. She liked it that she and Danny had a secret together, an inside joke. "Your house is very pretty," he said.

"Very pretty," Rick agreed. He looked right at her when he said it, but there was nothing flirtatious in his expression.

"But it should have trucks," Danny said.

"Trucks?" she asked. "In the kitchen? On the porch? On the roof?"

Danny smothered a giggle with both hands. "Not on the *roof*," he said.

"No, that would be silly," she agreed.

"In the driveway," he said. "They could go up and down the road. A dump truck and a fire truck and a cement mixer."

"A cement mixer? Wouldn't it be messy?"

"No, cement mixers are the best. Cement mixers are super cool."

"Oh, okay, if they're super cool…"

Rick was obviously enjoying Danny's happiness, watching him with amused pride. Her eyes stung with unshed tears, and this time the feeling was not selfish, not personal. These two had such a sweet, special bond, and it must be protected. She was glad she had chosen their side.

When they finished eating, Danny said, "Thank you for the lunch, Miss Scott," with his usual dutiful politeness and added, "It was dee-licious." She wanted to ask him to call her Jenna, but his father might not approve.

Rick said, "Thank you, Miss Scott," too, with the hint of a smile. She could not figure him out.

In the afternoon, Danny's energy flagged, and Rick put a drop cloth in the cab of the pickup so he could curl up and go to sleep. He put a sunshade on the windshield and left both doors standing open, but Jenna didn't think it could be very comfortable. She wanted to suggest he bring him into the house, but no—it wasn't her responsibility. She had provided lunch. If he wanted anything else from her, he would have to ask. Later Danny was running around the yard when he wasn't sitting on the steps with a book.

When Rick was finished painting, Danny helped him carry equipment to the pickup and chatted happily while they cleaned up. She went out on the porch to say goodbye. Rick said, "I'll be back Monday to do the trim."

She just nodded, but to Danny she said, "Thank you for helping. *Hasta la vista.*" She met Rick's gaze with her chin up. He was Danny's father, but he couldn't tell *her* what language to speak.

As he climbed into the truck, Danny said, "I like Miss Scott. She's super nice." Rick had nothing to say on the subject.

****

While she was making her solitary dinner, Rosalie called to ask if she had heard that the ground war had begun. She hadn't and didn't want to. Ever so casually, Rosalie asked how the painting was going. "Fine," Jenna told her. "It's almost done. He's doing a very good job. I'll be glad to have it finished." Rosalie didn't mention the rumors or the murder case, but her voice had a cautious tone, as if the children were listening.

Jenna went to bed a little early and woke up sometime in the night from a disturbing dream...physically disturbing. She couldn't remember any details, but one image lingered—Rick Alvarez, as he had looked standing in the sunshine in her yard with his shirt off. Damn the man! He was in her yard, in her house, in her life—he could at least stay out of her dreams! She did not want a man in her life now, not even in her dreams, and she most certainly didn't want him, with his perfect biceps and his thick black hair and his cute little son, disturbing her sleep, disturbing her life. Patrick had thought he was Rhett Butler. No doubt this guy thought he was...

Oh, stop it, Jenna! It wasn't as if he had asked her to dream about him. He had kissed her, though. He'd better not be dreaming about her! It was intolerable to think that when he looked at her with a slight smile and said, "Thank you, Miss Scott," he might have been remembering something he had dreamed or imagined about her.

He wouldn't try anything on Monday if he wanted to get paid. He had been genuinely shocked when she implied he might expect to take it out in trade. Exactly how much did she owe him? When the painting was finished, she needn't hire him ever again, but it would be difficult in a place like San Ignacio to avoid him altogether. He might have to leave town because the gossip would keep anyone else from hiring him, and she would never see him again. She would never see Danny again, either, and she would miss his innocent friendship.

It was a dream. Get over it! Aside from the kiss and his earnest apology, everything that had passed between them had been casual and friendly. Or at least it had been on his part; she had been a little bit rude to him—"prickly" he called it—and now she was blaming him for her dream. Just because she didn't know what he was thinking didn't mean he was doing anything wrong. She was as bad as the gossips.

She finally succumbed to sleep and did not dream again.

Chapter Nine

Sunday, February 24: Gen. Norman Schwarzkopf hails first day of allied ground offensive as "dramatic success."

Sunday morning Jenna slept late, ate a big breakfast, and took a leisurely stroll along the harbor. No painting would be done today, and much of San Ignacio was in church. Would it shame them into more charitable views or give them another gathering place for gossip? Rick had said "not today" when she asked if he attended church—would he go today and meet hostile stares and awkward silences? Had anybody told him what she couldn't?

She was walking slowly back to the house when Nancy came running over as so often before. She looked unhappy. Still sulky about the way Jenna had spoken to her? Or angry about something else? Something else. "Stupid old war," she grumbled. "There's nothing else on TV—all day and all night." She fell in beside Jenna, and they continued toward the house. "Boring!"

"Yes," she agreed, although it wasn't exactly the right word. The very idea made her skin crawl. Strong, healthy young men, expensively trained, the best of their generation, killing each other for no good reason—no reason was good enough.

"The 'raqis are running away."

"That sounds very smart of them. What have you been reading?"

"Nazis," Nancy said succinctly. She stopped in the path and waited for Jenna to turn back to face her. Her face was flushed, her eyes wary. She was unsure of what the reaction would be to the news she was bursting to tell.

"What?" Jenna asked. She had a sinking feeling in the pit of her stomach, as if she knew what was coming.

"Danny's father is in jail."

She didn't even consider whether it was true before she asked, "Where's Danny?"

Nancy shrugged. "He wasn't in Sunday school."

"Come on. I need to talk to your mother." She took the girl's hand, and they walked up the hill to the Hayes house. Rosalie might relish gossip, but she could also have facts. She was on good terms with Vince Allan.

Nancy led her in through the back door. The TV was on in the living room, a blur of serious words. Larry was slumped on the couch, staring at the screen. He glared at her resentfully and said nothing. He looked haggard and miserable, and the flickering images threw an unhealthy light on his face. Mike was watching too, leaning forward, elbows on knees.

Rosalie mildly reprimanded Nancy for repeating gossip and sent her back outside before she drew Jenna with her into the kitchen, away from the war talk. Rosalie was calm and sympathetic, no light of malice in her eyes. "He's not in jail," she assured her. "He wasn't arrested. Vince took him in for questioning, that's all." Not "asked him to come in," but "took him in," which sounded much more ominous. Or had she been careless in her choice of words or exaggerated for effect? Had Violet been "taken in" when she was questioned about the cabin?

"And—"

Rosalie shrugged. "That's all I know."

"Did he question anybody else?"

"Not that I know of."

"So why Rick? Why Rick first?" Anger was building in her. "Was there a reason? Evidence? Or was it the stupid gossip? The police aren't supposed to act on rumors!"

"Sit down. I'll make you a cup of coffee."

But Jenna couldn't sit down; she didn't want coffee; she didn't want to stay. She was so angry and so deeply, deeply sorry she hadn't warned him, hadn't given him a chance to defend himself. She rushed home and sat down in the outdated kitchen of her freshly painted house and wept.

****

It was after dark when she heard the pickup in the driveway. She didn't know what to think—her body was immediately thrown into crisis mode, her heart pounding. She hurried to the door, and Rick came up the steps. The moon, only days from full, made the porch light unnecessary. "Don't unlock the screen," he said. "I don't want to scare you." It seemed a very strange beginning. "I just wanted to ask you a question—one question."

"What is it?"

"Do you believe I killed Barbara Raymond?"

"No," she said and was glad of the conviction in her voice.

"Then why do they?" He wasn't asking her; he

turned away, asking himself. Out of everyone in San Ignacio, he had come to ask her this question, as if her opinion held great weight.

"Rick!" She reached for the latch. "Don't go. Come in—please." *Smart choice, Jenna, let the killer in.* Was it vampires who couldn't come in unless you invited them?

"No, I—"

"Please. We should talk about this."

He took a few seconds to decide, but he came back up the steps. She opened the door and led the way into the kitchen.

"Sit down," she said. "I'll make coffee." She didn't suppose either of them would sleep much tonight anyway.

He didn't sit down. "Do you know what happened?" he asked.

She shook her head, not sure what the question covered. "Where's Danny?" she asked.

"Heather Kelly is babysitting," he said. "He was scared, but he's okay."

"I'm sorry," she said, as if she were personally responsible for Danny's anguish. "Sit down, please."

"I was blindsided," he said, and Jenna winced. She should have told him—she couldn't imagine what the conversation would have been like, but she shouldn't have been such a coward.

"Rick," she said. "Sit down." He took a seat at the kitchen table, and she paused to light the burner under the teakettle.

"Vince Allan was nice about it," he said. "He said there was no evidence yet; it was all speculation, but everybody was talking about it. I guess he had to...go through the motions. It seems I was the last to know. Did you know?"

"Yes," she confessed.

"And you didn't tell me?"

Her face flushed with heat. "I—"

"No, no, I get it. I haven't been your favorite person." Yet he had sought out her opinion. Because she was new here, the outsiders sticking together? "Jenna, come here—sit."

"The coffee…"

"Never mind. Sit down, talk to me." She left the cups on the counter and sat down across from him. "I didn't even know Barbara Raymond," he said. "I met her at the barbecue. We didn't exchange two sentences. I didn't know her from Adam—she was nothing to do with me. Why the hell does everybody think I killed her?"

"I don't know. I don't know who started the rumor."

"Vince asked me if I'd slept with her. He said she'd had sex, apparently consensual, before she was murdered. Whoever that was—he might not have been the killer—it sure as hell wasn't me. Vince asked if I'd take a DNA test."

"That will clear you, won't it?"

"Yes, but the samples have to go to a lab in Sacramento. It takes weeks. In the meantime, my…neighbors believe this, and a fancy new forensics test won't change their minds. And Vince took my knife, my best carving knife."

Jenna thought of the sleeping kitten on her bedside table and bristled. "Did he have a warrant?"

"He didn't need one. I have nothing to hide."

"Do you have an alibi?"

"Only my son, who was asleep. Vince might have questioned every guy at the barbecue; sooner or later he would have gotten around to me—but he didn't. I was first on the list." His eyes met hers. "Tell me why. Tell me what they said."

"Oh, a lot of things, stupid things. You were both from L.A. I can't remember them all—I couldn't believe they were serious. What you said about her at the barbecue."

"What did I say?"

"You don't remember?"

"I remember you ladies were taking her apart. Maybe one of you killed her."

"You said, 'She's too beautiful. Women like that are nothing but trouble.' "

"And so she was," he said. "What else?"

"What does it matter? It was just stupid gossip, rumors. They'll be ashamed when they come to their senses."

"But they believed it—all of them, everybody. My so-called neighbors."

"Not everybody," Jenna protested. "I didn't. Rosalie said she didn't. Even if they repeated the rumors, it doesn't mean they believe them. I'm sure there are others who don't. The Kellys, if they let Heather babysit."

"She said they didn't want her to come, but she wouldn't disappoint Danny. He likes her to read to him. I was supposed to play poker with Harvey and Phil and Jeff, and they cancelled." So the damage had gone beyond words. The life he had made here was unraveling. Three years of living and working with these people, growing more confident of belonging here, and now the door had been slammed in his face, and he was an outsider after all.

"Heather must not have believed it."

"I didn't ask her. She's a kid. She'd been crying. Other people are getting hurt in this. Tell me why."

She shrugged. "You know them better than I do."

"I thought I did. Nobody told me what was going on. They talked to you—"

"I don't know why, Rick. They're just scared."

"Yes, of me," he said. "Do you know how that feels, to have people distrust you for no reason?"

Was he talking about racism now? If he wasn't, she was when she said, "It must have its uses, though—nobody will mess with you."

"They're messing with me now," he said. "Who did you talk to?"

Jenna shook her head; she didn't want to be responsible for directing his anger toward anybody in particular, although she might have cheerfully thrown Charlene Dickens to the wolves. "Does Gabe Burrows have something against you?" she asked instead.

"No," he said. "He just doesn't like anybody very much. He would be the first to believe anything negative, and he might repeat it, but he wouldn't have started it."

"You know who might have?" she said. "The real killer."

"Which means it's somebody we know," he said. "Not a stranger from L.A."

"I asked who started the rumors," she said, "but nobody knew—or cared."

"What else did they say?"

She tried to think. "Oh—somebody said they'd seen your pickup at her cabin."

"Right," he said. He seemed almost relieved. Here was something concrete, something he could defend himself against. "I fixed her broken window, but I dealt with Violet, not the renter. I never even saw the Raymond woman. My fingerprints would only be around the window and the front door. What else?"

"I don't remember," Jenna said, searching her memory. "You don't wear a wedding ring…"

"Oh, that's a good one," he said. At least he hadn't lost his sense of humor.

"No, it was…" She caught her breath. She hadn't meant to get into this. She was afraid to say it, physically afraid.

"What?" he asked. "Tell me."

"They—they said you killed your wife."

"Oh, my God," he said, and his tone was not at all what she had expected—not shock, outrage, grief, or guilt, but simple contempt for such credulity. "How long have they believed *that*, when they could have found out the truth so easily? Did *you* believe it?" he asked.

"No," she said. "Nancy—she was repeating something she heard at school—she said Danny's mother was murdered, and Rosalie said it wasn't true."

"Oh, it's true," he said. "She was murdered. Yes, Danny's mother was murdered. It's not a secret; it's public record. But I was never a suspect. There wasn't any mystery about who did it, believe me. The police knew who it was. They knew exactly what happened, because the bastards confessed." He stood up, shoving the chair aside.

"You don't have to…" she began. She didn't want to hear.

But once started, he couldn't seem to stop, the words spilling out in a rush, vivid and frightening. He wasn't looking at her. "They confessed," he repeated. "Hell, they bragged about it. There were two of them. Two big, ugly, stupid, skinhead sons of bitches. One of them was an off-duty cop. They were stinking drunk. They ambushed her in the parking lot. They raped her, and she fought—she broke one bastard's nose. And they…" He gestured with his right hand as if he held a knife. "They cut her. They stood there and watched her bleed to death and they called her…whore, spic whore… She was a good person, a strong, beautiful woman, somebody's wife, somebody's mother, and the best they could think of to do was to waste her life and let her know before she died that they thought she was nothing. I will *never* be able to forgive them."

"Why would you even try?" Jenna asked tearfully. Who had suggested he should? He did look at her then, and she must have looked as horrified as she felt.

"Oh, God, I'm sorry," he said. "I didn't mean to—" He turned to the stove and shut off the burner under the whistling teakettle. Jenna hadn't even noticed the sound. He took a few steps toward the door. Was he leaving?

She got up and approached him, thinking she should give him a quick, neighborly hug, to comfort him, to keep him there, to say—what? Some stupid cliché, "I'm sorry for your loss"? Instead she put both hands on his chest as if to push him away or to steady herself. He was still short of breath after the rush of words. What was her excuse? He was warm and solid and real under her fingers. It was not a dream, then, this feeling. Somehow her hands were on his shoulders, and she lifted her face to his.

This time the kiss was very mutual. Was it just sympathy, or had this powerful attraction existed all along? Either way, she was not stupid enough to think this was a good idea, but she let him take her face in his hands. His fingers explored as a blind man's would and brushed across her lips.

He kissed her again, a deeply sensuous kiss, and his hands caressed her neck and shoulders. He touched her breasts, lightly and through two layers of fabric, but it was enough, and Jenna felt both a shiver of pleasure and a stab of claustrophobic panic. She stiffened and caught her breath sharply.

"Do you want me to stop?" he asked, his voice husky.

"No," she said, but faintly. *Yes. God, yes.*

"Just tell me," he said. "*Now* would be a good time."

"No." She was glad he had asked, though. She wasn't about to be raped by Barbara Raymond's killer. No, she wasn't afraid of what he would do, but of what he could make her do—or feel. She didn't want to be hurt again as Patrick had hurt her.

Rick was holding her close now, kissing her sweetly. He paused as if to get his bearings, and then they drifted toward the bedroom, not in a hurry, but with a calm inevitability. In the doorway she heard herself whimper in protest. She didn't want to make love in her grandparents' antique four-poster. Yes, she did, but she didn't want to lie awake afterward and regret it.

The shutters were open, the room half flooded with moonlight. She was trembling with desire and with fear. He was a stranger, so unfamiliar in her arms, so overwhelmingly not Patrick, and yet here he was in her bedroom, undressing her. His hands were sure and gentle, and he took his time, not fumbling with buttons or hooks, all part of a silent ritual, with no need for words. He didn't seem to want any help, but when he had his boots off, she unbuttoned his shirt with fingers made clumsy by haste. He was in no hurry at all.

She lay back on the bed, and he approached her with gentle confidence. She took his head in her hands, stroked those beautiful cheekbones, and ran her fingers through his thick hair. "Enrique," she whispered. Another delicious, thrilling kiss, and his hands were on her face, her throat, her breasts, and still, even though his breathing was unsteady, every motion was calm and purposeful.

Hadn't she known, since the first time she saw him smile at Danny, that he was capable of this tenderness, of awakening this tenderness in her? Now he was kissing her bare skin and *oh—oh, God!*—touching her in ways she had never been touched, making every nerve end in her body stand at attention.

She was beyond ready when he said, "Jenna?" softly, awaiting her mute assent, and he was inside her, part of her, and everything was as easy and natural as breathing, as if they had always been together. She hadn't known this was possible—this patience, this generous sweetness. His mouth was on hers, and she was letting go of fear, beginning to trust him, and her thoughts scattered into pure feeling.

Revelation: Making love—it was not a euphemism

after all; *this* was what the words meant—lovemaking, the making of love…

****

Jenna awoke in her grandparents' bed in the silent darkness. Without consulting the clock, she knew it was nowhere near morning, and Rick was gone. Disappointment chilled her, but it was not as if he had chosen not to stay. He had Danny; he had to take Heather home. What she had missed most about marriage was simply being held, warm and comfortable, in bed. Would she ever have that again? Hadn't he kissed her before he left and said—what? No words would come. Was it all a dream?

Perhaps it was better that he had gone. She needed to be alone, to think, to sort out her feelings and put this in perspective. She lay awake for a long time, her mind a tangle. She felt as if she had been sleepwalking for the last few months and now she was awake. Ah, yes, *Sleeping Beauty*, with Rick Alvarez cast as Prince Charming. She might be happier if he left town right now and didn't spoil everything with words or second thoughts. Would he do that, let them run him out of town? Was she even a person in this, or had he merely sought comfort in the nearest warm body? She had known him less than two weeks. *Did* she know him? Would she never remember that middle-of-the-night impressions were always disproportionate?

Chapter Ten

Monday, February 25: U.S. officials report four U.S. soldiers killed, 21 wounded in first two days of allied ground assault; nearly 20,000 Iraqis taken prisoner; 270 tanks destroyed.

Jenna overslept and got up in a hurry, no time to lie in bed dreaming. In the shower, she had a strong feeling of horror for the stupid, dangerous mistake she had made—sleeping with a stranger—and yet she regretted washing away every trace of his touch. It might have meant nothing to him, but last night he had made her feel—oh, so much.

Was Nancy right? Was love making her stupid? No, this was not about love. She no longer believed in love. It was such incredible egotism to expect to be loved. She didn't know what last night had meant to him, or to her, but maybe she didn't need to know. One thing she did know: Patrick, whose ardor was only impatience, was not the great lover he imagined himself to be.

She wasn't even dressed yet when she heard a car stop on the road. She hurried to put on her robe—at least it was a nice one, a flattering soft blue. He had been in her bed last night; it was too late to be modest. She went to the door, wrapping a towel around her damp hair.

The pickup hadn't come up the driveway, but was stopped across the end of it. Danny was coming up the path with something in his hand. Jenna opened the door. She couldn't see Rick in the pickup. She never wanted to see him again and couldn't wait to see him. She met Danny on the porch. He smiled shyly and held out a ragged bouquet of wildflowers. "Hi, Miss Scott."

"Hi, Danny," she said. "*Buenos dias*." She took the flowers, delicate, fragrant blooms, with dew still on them. He smiled again, ran back down the driveway, and climbed into the pickup, which pulled away at once.

Okay, Danny had to go to school. She went back inside and put the bouquet in a glass of water and set it on the kitchen table. Flowers were a nice touch, but what did they mean? She dressed slowly, giving the process more attention than she had in some time. She chose a blue-and-green patterned blouse with a soft, open collar and tiny pearl buttons, and a pretty but practical denim skirt. She brushed her hair carefully, meeting her own eyes gravely in the mirror. She remembered Rick asking, "What do you call that color?" and how she had puzzled over the meaning of the question. Last night his hands had been in her hair. She hadn't put on any makeup, but there was a flush of pink in her cheeks.

She heard the crunch of tires on gravel as the pickup returned and parked in the turnaround as usual on a workday. She took a deep breath and stepped out on the porch. It was a moment before he got out of the pickup. She had never seen him hesitate before—another first. He wasn't dressed for painting but in the black jeans and T-shirt he had worn when he worked on the roof. She missed the tool belt. He walked slowly up the path. Yes, he would take his time now, when she was on tenterhooks. Her feelings were a mixture of exasperation, dread, concern, eagerness, and simple joy. Would he be glib about last night…or worse? She braced herself not to overreact to whatever he would have to say.

He met her eyes as he climbed the steps. He looked—well, he looked gorgeous, but as if he hadn't slept much. Could she have rocked his world too? Did he have feelings as confused as hers? "Are you okay?" he asked.

Jenna nodded. "Danny's all right?" she asked, her throat tight.

"He wanted to go to school. That's the hardest part about being a parent—letting him go. I asked Miss Lacey, his teacher, to make sure nobody gave him a hard time. She said she would, but if looks could kill…" Yes, of course he was still preoccupied with the rumors and the welfare of his son. He had enough on his mind without thinking of her.

"Does he know you were here last night?" she asked.

He shook his head.

"Come on in," she said and led the way. "Have you had breakfast?"

He didn't answer. He didn't seem to know.

"Rick?" she said. "Breakfast? It's an easy question."

"Danny had cereal," he said. Perhaps he thought she was questioning his parenting skills.

"Come on," she said. "You need to eat." They had arrived in the kitchen, and he noticed the flowers on the table. "They're very sweet," she said. "Are they from you or Danny?"

"Both," he said, but added, with an air of confession, "It was Danny's idea. He thinks I should marry you."

"Bless his heart," Jenna said. She tried not to imagine the conversation *that* would have come out of. "I'm sure he misses his mother—he's just trying to replace her."

"I don't want to…" He sounded irritated, but he let it go.

"Sit down," she said. "I'll make you a decent breakfast. I'm out of bacon, but I have sausage." She opened the refrigerator and took out eggs and milk.

"Jenna," he said, "I'm really sorry I said all that to you last night. There was no need for me to tell you the ugly details."

She set the food on the counter and faced him. "*That's* what you're sorry about?" she asked.

"Unless you're planning to make me sorry about something else," he said coolly. *Sorry if I was out of line.* But this time she had made the first move, and he had asked if she wanted to stop. He had availed himself of what she had offered, nothing more.

She returned to the refrigerator for bread and sausage. She put the sausage in her grandmother's cast iron skillet and lit the burner. She was glad to have a job to keep her hands occupied, an excuse not to look at him, but she also felt a certain pleasure in the simple task of giving him something to eat, engaging in ordinary domestic details on his behalf, like any other foolish, unliberated woman. She knew breakfast was her culinary strong suit.

The sizzle of browning sausage filled a silence that had gone on too long. Were they going to address the elephant in the room or not? She wouldn't say anything unless he did, and apparently he wasn't going to. He had mentioned the story he had told her last night, so she asked, "When was she killed—your wife?"

"Three years ago."

"Right before you moved here? What happened to the men who did it?" She was opposed to the death penalty, but open to making exceptions. Why was she asking for more details, when he had just apologized for what he'd already said?

"They made a plea bargain to avoid execution. Life, no possibility of parole. So we were spared a trial."

"Better for everyone," she agreed. "And then you and Danny came here?"

"I wasn't running away," he said. "I was trying to change our life for the better."

"What can I say?" she asked. "I *was* running away when I came here. But if I were you, my first instinct would be to move somewhere where there were no people like them."

"I did," he said and added, reluctantly, "or I thought I did."

"No," she said, "I meant…"

It took him a second. "Oh, you mean people who *look* like them? No, that was the mistake *they* made."

It was a gentle reproof, but Jenna blushed. She cracked eggs and began to beat them. "So now what?" she asked.

"Maybe Danny's right," he said. "Maybe I should marry you."

"What, for my French toast?" she joked, but no, he was serious. "Oh, Rick, to make an honest woman of me? It's 1991," she reminded him. And yet, as little as she knew him, as little as she wanted to be married to anyone ever again, as bruised as she still was by Patrick's desertion, she could imagine herself willingly, recklessly giving herself, body, heart, and soul, to this handsome stranger. Why? "I don't even know you," she said. "Anyway, technically I'm still married. My divorce isn't final yet."

"Oh!" She understood his surprise. As far as she knew, nobody in San Ignacio was aware of her marital status. She hoped he wasn't Catholic enough to believe they had committed adultery. While he absorbed the news, she made a decision to tell him her most humiliating truth.

"My husband left me," she said.

"Why?" he asked without hesitation. "Is he an idiot?"

Jenna laughed, and oh, it was good to laugh like that again. No matter what happened afterward—if he left town, spoke of this in hurtful ways, spread rumors about her, ignored her, lied to her, gave her a disease, hit her, got her pregnant, cheated on her, broke her heart, proved to have murdered Barbara Raymond—she knew she would always be grateful to him for this moment.

"I guess so," she said. "He left me for a skinny blonde girl younger than me."

"Younger than you? You're what—twenty?"

"Twenty-five." *Flatterer*. Or was that a comment on how little she had learned from Patrick?

"Definitely an idiot," he said. She looked at him,

laughing, and he responded with his dazzling smile.

"That's better," she said. "So where do we go from here?"

"I have no idea," he said. "Wherever you want to go. Would you like me to break your husband's neck?"

She laughed again. "No, better not. I'm not really this kind of girl, I'll have you know. We got carried away last night, but nobody's marrying anybody here. They say trying to rush a relationship is one of the signs of an abuser, and I don't want to go from a cheater to an abuser."

"An abuser?" Apparently that stung, but he said, "Okay, whatever you want. If you need me to back off, I will."

"What about you? Considering what happened, three years is not a long time to grieve."

"I'm still grieving," he said matter-of-factly, "but life goes on."

"Yes, it does," she said, "and in case you were wondering, last night was…" She hesitated, lest she be the one to spoil it with words, and settled on "perfect."

"You like dangerous men," he suggested.

"Are you dangerous?"

"Ask Barbara Raymond," he said. "You didn't like me at all until you thought I killed her."

"I never thought you killed her." At least not in daylight. "I didn't like you because you scared the hell out of me. You still do. If I hadn't seen the way you were with Danny, I would have had you arrested for sexual assault when you kissed me."

"Well, thank God for Danny," he said. "But you still don't trust me?"

She didn't. She didn't know if she would ever trust

him, if she would ever again completely trust any man, but for the first time since Patrick's betrayal, she wanted to try.

"You don't believe I murdered anyone?" he asked. "But you're afraid I'll—what, break your heart?"

"Will you?"

"I'll tell you what," he said. "If I do, you have my permission to shoot me."

"I don't have a gun," she said.

"I'll buy you one. When's your birthday?"

Jenna laughed. Who would have guessed this man, who had seemed so grim and forbidding to her at first, would turn out to be someone who could make her laugh? At the risk of too serious a discussion, she asked, "Were you a good husband?"

"You'd have to ask her," he said and sobered. "I didn't cheat, but I never took her to Paris."

"Paris is overrated," she said. "I'm sure you kept the house in good repair."

"We lived in an apartment. I painted the nursery—Danny's room. She wanted turquoise, but I drew the line." She heard a trace of wistfulness in his voice, as if he wanted to take back the refusal. "And then...I wasn't there when she needed me most." He spoke with simple regret. He would never forgive the bastards who had killed her, but perhaps he had forgiven himself.

"Where were you?" She was a little ashamed of her curiosity.

"I was at home. I was with Danny. She had an evening class. If I had driven her to school and picked her up...I told her to always park under the lights." He shook his head. "Sorry, I know I shouldn't dwell on that. I have better memories."

"How long were you married?"

"Six years."

"Did you remember your anniversaries?"

"Every one, but I don't deserve much credit. We got married on the Fourth of July."

"Oh, that was clever. Does Danny remember her?" She set a plate of sausage and French toast in front of him.

"Yes. I'm not sure how much."

She poured the coffee and sat down across from him. "Tell me about her," she urged. She is not my rival, she reminded herself. She gave him Danny. She taught him how to love. He had said she was strong and beautiful—why, then, would he be attracted to somebody as unexceptional as Jenna Scott?

"She—her name was Celia." He gave it a very Spanish pronunciation: SAY-lee-ah.

There, she thought, all anybody had to do was ask about her.

"She was very smart. She was a terrific mom. She was like Danny—mostly sunny."

"Not prickly like me?"

"She's gone, Jenna. This is a different chapter." So no comparisons were to be made? "What about your husband?" he asked.

"Ex-husband. Patrick. Patrick Callahan. He's a jerk," she said, adding with a sudden rush of understanding, "He's a silly, stupid boy. He's not important. He didn't deserve me."

"Obviously not. You didn't take his name?"

"I didn't keep it," she said, and an image flashed unbidden in her mind: *Jenna Alvarez.*

"This is very good," he said. "Did you put

cinnamon in it?" Oh, yes, breakfast. She was forgetting to eat.

"Yes, a little cinnamon. Do you want orange juice?"

He didn't.

Presently she remembered something else. "Are you planning to leave town—because of the rumors?"

"No," he said grimly. "Not unless I can't make a living," which of course was a real possibility.

"Good," she said. "Because my house still needs painting."

"Oh, yes, sure," he said. "I can finish the trim today."

"Not dressed like that," she said. "You don't want to get paint on your shirt."

"Oh, sorry, I wasn't thinking about work this morning. I'll go home and change."

"You're not very professional," she chided. "You never even gave me an estimate."

"I know," he said. "I didn't want to give you an excuse to change your mind."

"What about the discount? Did you make up the story about owing my grandfather?"

"I don't make things up," he said.

"So…why did you owe him?" She expected a story about how her grandfather helped him out in the beginning by loaning him money or making referrals for him.

"He left the house to his granddaughter," he said.

"You mean—instead of developers or undesirable outsiders?"

"No, I mean to you."

She was a little slow on the uptake. "Oh, and I'm

so irresistible," she said.

"Something like that," he agreed.

"Seriously, Rick…"

"Seriously, Jenna."

She felt her neck and ears get hot. "You might have asked me out."

"You were a little standoffish," he pointed out. "I didn't think you'd want to go out with the hired help."

"You're not hired help. You're an independent contractor."

"Jack of all trades," he said. "Master of none."

"I beg to differ," she said and blushed again.

When they had finished eating, she got up to put the dishes in the sink, and he got up too. Was he ready to leave? He carried the empty coffee cups to the counter and put his hand on the back of her neck. Jenna dropped a fork in the sink with a loud clatter. Was this his idea of backing off? He lifted her hair and kissed the nape of her neck, a spot he had missed last night. "Behave yourself, Enrique," she said. He pulled her into his arms. "Does anyone call you that?" she asked.

"Not here," he said and kissed her forehead.

"But in L.A.? Did your wife?" She closed her eyes, giving in to a rising tide of feeling.

"Yes." He kissed her closed eyelids.

"So would you rather I didn't?" she asked.

"You can call me anything you like," he said. "Just shut up when I'm trying to kiss you." No, he wasn't leaving yet.

He kissed her mouth, not aggressively but sweetly and as thoroughly as she had ever been kissed. It took a while. When she could breathe, she said, "Anybody ever tell you you're a great kisser?"

Linda Griffin

"Oh, sure," he said. "Barbara Raymond."

"Not funny," she said, but she laughed anyway. "Am I going to be able to get any work done today?" she asked. "I do have a deadline."

"Not right now," he said. He undid the top button of the blouse she had chosen for him. "This is very pretty," he said, touching the fabric, touching her.

"What if someone comes?" Nancy was safely in school. Considering the rumors, would Rosalie barge in if she saw the pickup?

"Lock the door," he said.

In the bedroom, as he undid the pearl buttons—and there were a lot of them—she complained, "I just put this *on*."

"Sorry," he said, laughing. It was a lovely beginning, laughter. They were friends now, not strangers. They knew each other's secrets and had room for playfulness.

The eerie moonlight and shadows of the night before had been replaced by bright sunlight. She knew her every flaw must be revealed, but he touched her with his gaze and his hands with something so like reverence that self-consciousness vanished. He made her feel beautiful, cherished. He *was* beautiful: his smiling eyes, his capable hands, his warm brown skin...

"Breathe, Jenna," he said teasingly, the intent silence of last night only a haunting memory. "Tell me what you like," he urged, although he certainly wasn't waiting for instructions.

It was just as before, in all the best ways, and it was completely different.

****

Rick was sitting on the edge of the bed, shirtless,

118

putting on his boots, with Jenna propped up against the pillows behind him, when he spotted the small carving on the bedside table. "Where did you get that?" he asked.

She ran her hand down his back and kissed his shoulder. She was on the edge of something that felt like hope. "I bought it from Megan," she said.

"When?"

"Friday. Right after I heard the rumors."

"Damn!" He leaned back to give her a kiss. "You are something, Jenna Scott."

He picked up the carving, and she took it out of his hand. She ran a finger along the gentle curve of the kitten's back. "It's lovely," she said. "It's so real; you must have taken it from life. Do you have a cat?" She knew nothing about him. She had never even been inside his house. She had been too self-involved to learn the first thing about him.

"Danny has a cat," he said, watching her stroke the smooth wood. "Or the cat has Danny. She comes and goes as she pleases."

She liked that. "Does she have a name?"

"Danny named her Señorita. His mom was teaching him Spanish."

Okay, she *had* been curious about one or two things. "Is that why you don't want him to speak it?"

"I never said I didn't," he said, surprised. "I'd like him to be bilingual. We—"

"When you worked on the roof," she reminded him.

"What? Oh, no, I just wanted him to remember to use English with—"

"Stupid Anglo women?"

He gave her a look, not quite amused, not quite disapproving. "—people who might not understand Spanish. And you were so scornful with 'This is California, Mr. Alvarez.' Like I said, irresistible."

"You just like a challenge," she said.

****

Eventually they had to return to the real world. Rick was heading home to change into his painting clothes, and she went out on the porch with him, her fingers linked in his. It was a nice day, sunny and only a little bit cold.

He stopped abruptly and let go of her hand. He gestured wordlessly toward the pickup. The tailgate was down, which it surely hadn't been when he came in. He strode quickly to the turnaround, Jenna trailing behind. Bright spots of green paint dotted the gravel. One of the cans in the pickup bed was open, a brush protruding from the top.

He walked around to the driver's side, and she followed. Painted across the full length of the pickup, in large dark green letters against the gray metal, was a single word:

KILLER

Jenna gasped. "Should I call the police?" she asked.

"No," he said. "Go in the house and lock the door."

"Why?" she asked.

"We didn't hear a car. Whoever did this might have been on foot. He might still be around."

She shook her head. "We might not have heard the car, and this is the act of a coward. I'm not afraid." She was, though. Who would have done such a thing? Was this a childish prank, the senseless act of a hatemonger,

120

or perhaps the murderer, trying to throw further suspicion on Rick?

"Okay," he said. "I won't be long." He closed the tailgate and handed her the open can of paint. She held the handle gingerly—wouldn't there be fingerprints? He cupped her chin in his hand and kissed her, and for the first time she understood that this was serious, that he meant their connection to be real. Lovemaking, however skillful, however deeply felt, couldn't promise as much as this casual, possessive, half-distracted goodbye kiss.

Her eyes stung with tears. "What are you going to do?" she asked, gesturing at the defaced pickup.

"I think I'll keep it," he said. "I like it," but he got into the cab and slammed the door hard.

While he was gone, Jenna retrieved her sketchbook and studied the drawing she had made—was it only eight days ago?—when she sat on the porch while he showed Nancy how to scrape paint. It was a very poor likeness. She knew she could never do him justice in any case. What had bothered her about his face when she drew this? Whatever it was, she couldn't see it now. Hadn't she thought his nose was too wide? It wasn't, of course; it was perfect—and he didn't go around sticking it into other people's business!

He drove back about ten minutes later. He parked the pickup as he had before, with the ugly word facing the road. He was wearing his paint-spattered white clothing and set immediately to work arranging drop cloths and putting up the ladder. Jenna went out to give him the open can of paint. If he didn't plan to go to the police, the fingerprints didn't matter. "You're not really going to leave it like that?" she asked.

Linda Griffin

He was squeezing paint from the brush against the inside of the can and didn't look up. "It's only paint," he said. "Sticks and stones."

"But Danny," she said. "Won't he be upset?"

He hesitated, as if he meant to wear the word as a badge of honor and was reluctant to give it up. "Yes," he said finally. "I can probably get it off, but it will take a while. I'll paint over it before I pick him up. Kids change your whole world, you know?"

"I know," she said. Danny had already changed hers.

"Speaking of which," he said, "as much as Danny might like a little sister, that wasn't what I had in mind when I came over here last night."

"Don't worry," she said. "I've got it covered." She didn't, but there was no point in his worrying about it now. She had to give him credit for raising the subject, even if it was a little late.

She returned to the house and worked a little on the illustrations, but her concentration was completely shattered. Rick worked steadily all morning. He kept his shirt on—the weather was cooler than it had been Friday—and he didn't whistle. He was doing the trim, which was careful, precise work, and she imagined he didn't want to be distracted.

While she struggled to work, she remembered the first day she had gone into Sam's Grocery and Violet had come in with her loud voice and big heart. *Anybody doesn't treat you right, you let me know. We don't put up with any nonsense in San Ignacio.* She put down her pencil and went into the kitchen. She had shoved the thin local phone directory into a drawer. The information was a bit outdated, but Violet's number

122

wouldn't have changed. She picked up the phone, confident that whatever could be done about the rumors would be done. Rick didn't have to know.

At lunchtime she went out, and he was cleaning up. "Are you finished?" she asked.

"Yes," he said without enthusiasm. "Take a look." She walked around and surveyed the entire house. It looked so much better than it had when she arrived, fresh and clean and bright. She had made a good choice in the trim color, but now it seemed almost sinister, a vandal's medium.

"Thank you," she said and gave him a kiss. "You did a beautiful job. Don't forget to give me a bill." He shook his head. "I know—awkward," she said. "But business is business." Which, of course, was why sleeping with your contractor wasn't a good idea. He couldn't accept payment, or she free services. "Come in and have lunch."

He hesitated, but there were only a few spatters of drying green paint on his shirt, so he agreed and followed her in. He sat at the table, and she busied herself with lunch preparations. "I'll put the screens back up tomorrow," he said. He sounded tired, and Jenna didn't know what to say that might help. What if most of his customers stopped hiring him because they believed he was responsible for Mrs. Raymond's death? They had joked about her earlier, but it wasn't funny now. Words exchanged in Sam's Grocery were now made visible in dark green paint. Might even the police come to believe them, when he had no alibi? Was he in real danger?

"Rick," she said. "Did you say you fixed a broken window at Mrs. Raymond's cabin?"

"Yes, why?"

"How did it get broken? Could it have had something to do with her murder?"

"I don't think so. Violet said some kids were throwing rocks."

"Did you see a rock?"

"No. Are you playing Nancy Drew?"

"I'm trying," she said.

There was a knock at the front door, and a familiar voice called, "Jenna?"

"It's Rosalie," she said. She quickly took the kitchen drawing down from its place near the sink and handed it to Rick. "Come in," she called. "We're in the kitchen."

When Rosalie entered, they were sitting on opposite sides of the table, the drawing spread out between them. If she had come down the hill from her house, she would have seen the pickup and shouldn't be surprised he was there, but she stopped when she saw him, looking embarrassed.

"Hi," Jenna said. "Come see Rick's plan for my kitchen."

"Hi," Rosalie said tonelessly. She didn't even glance at the drawing. She looked worried. "I don't want to interrupt…"

"Is something wrong?" Jenna asked.

"Have you seen Larry?"

"Isn't he in school?"

"They called and said he was absent this morning. He admired you—I thought maybe…"

"I haven't seen him. He played hooky?"

"It's not like him. But he's been very moody lately. He's been obsessed with the war, you know? He had a fight with Heather, and they usually get along so well."

"Do you know what the fight was about?" Jenna asked, wondering if it was about Rick.

"No, but they haven't been speaking. She says she hasn't seen him."

"Have you seen him today?" Jenna asked Rick.

"No," he said, "but I'll keep an eye out for him. Are you sure he didn't go out with Mike?" he asked Rosalie.

"Never on a school day," she said. "I won't allow it. He left the house as usual, and his bike is gone."

"He's probably just goofing off," Rick said, but with sympathy for her worry, one parent to another. "Do you want me to go hunt for him?"

"No!" she said a little too emphatically. "He—he wouldn't want you to. I thought he might come home for lunch, but he hasn't. If he doesn't show up soon, I'll call Vince, and if he does, I'm going to wring his neck." She tried to laugh, but she was too near tears. "I'd better go," she said.

Jenna got up and walked out with her. At the foot of the steps, Rosalie made an effort at calm and said, "The house looks great. Rick did a good job on the painting."

"Yes," Jenna said briskly, like any satisfied customer.

Rosalie, undeceived, gave her a knowing look. "Don't let him break your heart," she said.

"What? Don't be silly." More to distract her than anything else, she asked, "Did you see what they did to his truck?"

Rosalie stared at the pickup, puzzled. She wouldn't have seen the vandalism unless she had approached from the road. Jenna motioned for her to follow, and they walked around to the driver's side.

Rosalie shuddered, and her hand went to her throat.

"Ugly, isn't it? I thought life here was going to be peaceful."

"Did he call the police?" Rosalie asked tearfully.

"No. Are you okay?"

"Yes. I'd better get home. Larry might call or—"

"Let me know," Jenna said, and Rosalie hurried away.

She returned to the kitchen. "Is she all right?" Rick asked.

She shook her head. "Maybe I should go over there later. She said you did a good job on the house—and I shouldn't let you break my heart."

He was unperturbed. "She doesn't miss much," he said. "And I will buy you a gun."

She sighed. "Now that you've finished painting, you won't have a reason to come over," she said.

"Except the best one," he said. "And of course…" He held up the kitchen drawing.

"No, Rick—"

"It's not as if I've had a lot of requests for my services lately," he said.

"Maybe you would if you had a phone," she suggested.

"Bugs you, doesn't it?" He grinned.

It did. It was so nineteenth century. A man with a child should want to be easily contacted. Had there been a shattering phone call in the middle of the night—"I'm sorry, Mr. Alvarez. Your wife…"? No, surely they would make such notifications in person. There was no echo of tragedy here, only quiet stubbornness. It was a clue to his character. He might be equally unreasonable on other subjects. She still suspected hostility between him and Gabe Burrows. Hadn't he muttered something about Rick the day he put in her phone? She hadn't been sure even then and now couldn't remember what the words might have been.

"Who do you think vandalized the truck?" she asked. "Could it have been Gabe?"

Rick made a dismissive gesture. "He's a harmless old grouch," he said.

"You don't think he's a racist?" she asked.

"No." He sounded not offended but almost bored. "There's enough of that in the world. Don't go looking for it."

After lunch, he finished cleaning up and used the leftover green paint to obscure each letter on the pickup—adding still more to remove later—before he left to pick Danny up at school.

Jenna returned to her drafting table, feeling bereft. He had said he would be back tomorrow, but they had made no definite plans. They could not spend the night or even the evening together because of Danny. She didn't have to be told they couldn't raise a child's hopes of a lasting relationship until they were sure themselves. There were still a million things they didn't know about each other, any one of which might be a deal breaker.

She worked for a while, but soon gave up. She made a batch of cookies and took them up the hill to the Hayes house. Mike was still out fishing—he hadn't been told Larry was truant. Nancy was unusually subdued and stayed in her room doing homework.

Rosalie had called Vince Allan when Larry didn't come home after school let out. She alternated between anger and the verge of tears. "He's never done this before," she said. "He's always been a good boy." She sat on the couch and stared unseeing at the television, where reporters talked of the Iraqi army "advancing to the rear" and low battlefield casualties, although at least twenty American soldiers had been killed by a Scud missile in a Saudi barracks. Sickened, Jenna asked if she could turn it off. Rosalie shook her head. "Larry likes to keep track of it," she said vaguely.

Jenna helped her with dinner preparations and stayed until almost time for Mike to come home. "Call me if you hear anything," she said, "or if you need anything." She walked back down the hill and put together her own dinner—even angry and distracted, Rosalie had done better—and finally settled down to serious work.

It was nearly midnight when she went to bed, and Larry Hayes was still missing.

Chapter Eleven

Tuesday, February 26: Brig. Gen. Richard Neal in Riyadh, Saudi Arabia, says Iraqi forces are in "full retreat" with allied forces pursuing; Iraqi POWs number 30,000-plus.

Tuesday morning was cooler and overcast, the early spring weather put on hold. The ocean was choppy, the sky leaden.

Rick drove to Jenna's house after he dropped Danny at school. He was wearing black again and his tool belt. "You have no idea how sexy that getup is," she told him and gave him a kiss. "Are you working today?"

"I'll put the screens back up, but what I would like to do is take some more careful measurements of your kitchen. Then we could go to the city and look at materials and have lunch in a real restaurant. What kind of food do you like?"

"Mexican."

"Is that a joke?"

"No. Mexican or Italian. But I told you I can't do the kitchen right now. I haven't even paid for the painting."

"But it won't hurt to make plans," he said. "It might be fun."

"It might be expensive. Besides, it's two hours to

the city, and Larry is missing…"

"Still? I was sure he'd show up when school was over."

"He didn't. Rosalie called the police."

"Okay, so they'll have it covered. There's nothing we can do. If we go to the city—"

"Are you still trying to push me into remodeling the damn kitchen?"

He sighed. "No, Jenna, I am trying, in my own apparently ineffectual way, to ask you out on a date."

"Oh," she said.

"I'm afraid San Ignacio has limited entertainment options. The café isn't bad, if you like cheeseburgers, but we would be out of place at the teen hangout, and the movie theater is closed on weekdays this time of year." Yes, and people would talk, and there was always the possibility someone would say something to Rick about Barbara Raymond—or worse, his wife—or stare and whisper behind their backs. "There are other places to eat on the highway," he continued, "but they're all fast food for tourists—not what I had in mind. We could play pool at the tavern, or I could take you fishing…"

"And you told Nancy you weren't a romantic! Let's stay here until we know about Larry," she said. "But thank you, I'd love to have lunch in the city with you sometime."

He said he had eaten breakfast, and she had had oatmeal, so after he replaced the window screens they sat on the porch and drank coffee. The sharp, antiseptic smell of fresh paint was fading. The damp, fresh, salty air was a little too cool for her thin sweater, so he put his arm around her. They were sitting like that when

Rosalie slogged down the hill.

Jenna started to put distance between them, but changed her mind. It was too late to try to fool her neighbor, and she wouldn't notice much of anything right now. She looked completely exhausted.

"Oh, Rosalie, I'm so sorry," Jenna said. "Come sit down. Let me get you a cup of coffee."

She shook her head. "I've had too much already."

"There's been no word?" Rick asked.

"None. I'm afraid they'll find his body on the rocks like Mrs. Raymond," she said. Jenna couldn't say the possibility hadn't occurred to her, but hearing his mother say the words was awful.

"Is there anything we can do?" she asked.

"No, I just had to get away for a while. Mike and Nancy stayed home today, and they're driving me crazy. Mike is all macho about it, and Nancy won't…stop…talking." She sat down on the steps and put her head in her hands. Jenna put a comforting hand on her shoulder; it was all she could do.

"I could drive around and see if I can find him," Rick offered. "I know the police are searching, but…"

"No, you can't," Rosalie said. "Don't you see? He thinks you murdered Barbara Raymond. Mike does too. You're the last person we want out looking for him."

Rick swore under his breath and hugged Jenna closer.

"No, I know you didn't do it—I don't know why Mike is so convinced. Somebody else killed her, some lunatic, and now he has Larry."

"Oh, Rosalie!" Jenna couldn't think of anything else to say. She could not imagine how Rosalie could face such a possibility even for a second.

They were still sitting on the porch when a white car with beacon lights came down the road. It slowed as it passed, as if it was about to stop next door. A bicycle was mounted on the rack at the back. Rosalie stood up with a terrified cry and started to run up the hill.

"No, wait!" Rick called. "He's turning around."

Yes, the police car had made a U-turn and was coming back, up the driveway. Apparently the driver had seen them in front of the house. Jenna rushed to Rosalie's side and held her still where she was, and Rick walked slowly toward the car.

The man who got out of the driver's seat was about fifty, heavyset, with a mustache and gray at his temples. "Vince," Rick said.

"Rick," said Chief Allan. He nodded toward the pickup. "Interesting paint job." He tipped his hat to the ladies and opened the back door of the police car. They could all see a teenage boy sitting in the back seat, head down. It was Larry Hayes.

Rosalie broke free and would have run to him, but Allan held up a hand. "He's okay, Rosie. You can take him home in a few minutes," he said. "I found him up at Violet's cabins. He'd been there all night."

"Barbara Raymond's cabin," Rick guessed.

"The very one. We don't have to wait for the DNA tests—he admits to having sex with her."

Rosalie gasped. "Larry? He's only sixteen! You're not saying he killed her?"

"Oh, my God," Jenna said. She remembered him at the barbecue, offering her a plate of food, bristling with newfound masculinity in Rick's presence, taking offense at her remarks about the war, and stalking off to flirt with Mrs. Raymond. Jenna had humiliated him, and in front of a man he measured himself against. "It's my fault," she said, stunned. With a few careless words, had she transformed this boy into a murderer?

But Vince Allan shook his head.

"Yes!" Larry said, climbing out of the car. His clothes and hair were disheveled, his face tear-streaked, and the look in his eyes frankly murderous. Across the front of his shirt were scattered telltale specks of dark green paint. "It *is* your fault!" he yelled at Jenna. "You stuck-up bitch, you think you're better than everybody else. You treated me like a baby! Mrs. Raymond didn't think I was such a kid. She wanted me!"

"Larry!" Rosalie said sharply, and he fell silent.

"Apologize," Rick said in the firm, gentle tone he might have used to Danny. "Apologize to Miss Scott, and to your mother for worrying her."

Larry sneered. "Oh, yeah? Who's gonna make me—you?"

"Nobody should have to make you do anything," Vince Allan said reasonably. "You're old enough to be responsible for your own actions."

Larry faltered. "Sorry," he said grudgingly. He didn't look at Jenna.

Vince continued in a brisk, businesslike tone, "The only charges we have pending are for trespassing—that will be Violet's call—and vandalism." He looked at Rick.

"I don't care," Larry burst out. "Put me in jail. I'm not apologizing to *him*."

"No, but you'll pay to have the pickup repainted," Rosalie said. "Just be glad you're not being charged with murder."

"I didn't—" he began indignantly, and Allan

silenced him with a gesture.

"He was with Mrs. Raymond earlier that day, right after she left the barbecue."

"No," Rosalie said. "He was with his friends."

"No, he wasn't," Allan said. "He was with her, but he was home in bed when she was murdered."

"By *him*," Larry said, glaring at Rick. "He was jealous because she was with me, and now he's over here all the time with *her*."

"I didn't kill her, Larry. Who told you I did?'

"Everybody says it. Dad, everybody."

"So," Chief Allan said, regaining control of the situation. "Vandalism charges?"

Rick shook his head.

"Okay, Rosie, you can take him home." And to Larry, "Don't forget your bike."

Larry, still sullen, slouched back and lifted the bicycle off the rack and started pushing it up the hill. Rosalie, poised to follow, said, "Thank you, Rick. We'll take care of having the pickup repainted. If there's anything else I can do…"

"Try not listening to gossip," he said.

Rosalie, hurrying to catch up, was reading Larry the riot act. "I'm going to wring your neck!"

The police car pulled out, and Rick and Jenna went back to sit on the porch. She felt extremely fragile and was afraid she would disgrace herself by bursting into tears in front of him. What would he do if she did? Patrick had always hated it. What did Rick do when Danny cried? Regardless of who had killed Barbara Raymond, she had inadvertently set in motion this chain of events, which, she reminded herself, included the comfort they had taken in each other's arms.

Rick understood. She put her head on his shoulder, and he put his arm around her and kissed her temple, and when tears began, he brushed them away. "Not your fault," he murmured. Yes, Larry was responsible for his own actions, but still—she might have considered the consequences before she spoke so harshly to him. Now what might have been his first sexual experience would be forever linked to tragedy.

"Do you think he was right?" she asked. "The murderer was jealous because she was with him?"

"Maybe."

"Larry hates me," she said dismally. "Maybe the whole family. It's not going to be comfortable living next door."

"Come on," he said. He stood up and took her hand to pull her up beside him. "Show me your work."

It would not have occurred to her, but he was right. It would help her to focus on something positive, somewhere she had not failed. They went inside, and she laid out sheets for his inspection.

"These are amazing, Jenna," he said and asked intelligent questions to prove it wasn't idle flattery. "Do you have a degree?"

"MFA," she said. "But this is all just technical skill."

"Just?" he said. "The important thing is—do you enjoy it?"

"Sometimes. Yes. When you're not distracting me—you know, climbing around on my roof, taking your shirt off in my yard."

"Man, you are tough!" he said.

"But I wish I were better at the creative stuff."

"I liked the portrait you did of Nancy," he said.

"Thank you." Because he'd been so nice to her, she dug out her sketchbook and showed him the one she had done of him.

"Oh, ugh," he said, and they both laughed. He did know how to make her feel better.

They went back out on the porch, and when they had exhausted the subject of the still unknown murderer, told each other some of the things they needed to know if they were to have a future together.

He had never smoked, and although he had nothing against a beer or two on social occasions, he hadn't had one since Danny was born. He wasn't a gambler—very little money changed hands at the San Ignacio poker games—but he was a pretty good card player.

"I knew that one," she said. "Great poker face."

She already knew he was a loving father, punctual, and a hard worker. In short, he had no vices, no faults, unless she counted the baffling refusal to have a telephone, the inability to resist the urge to kiss Bill Scott's granddaughter, and of course his cardinal failing—he didn't like chocolate.

"What can I tell you?" he said. "I'm a pretty boring guy."

He was a lapsed Catholic and sometimes attended San Ignacio's nondenominational Protestant church. He was a registered independent voter with Democratic leanings. Most of his ancestors were from northern Mexico, but his family had been in the United States longer than hers. He had recently turned thirty-four, so she had missed his birthday. He rooted for the Los Angeles Dodgers but wouldn't hold it against Jenna that her father was a Yankees fan.

He didn't miss teaching; his present work suited

him better. His mother didn't want him to waste his education, but he didn't feel it was wasted.

"Education is never wasted," she put in.

His parents still lived in Los Angeles.

"And you never call them," she said.

"I write letters, Jenna."

"Are you going to tell them about me?"

"I already have."

"Did you tell them I…have red hair?"

"Auburn," he corrected. *Oh!* Was that what that was about?

"So they know I'm not Latina?"

"I think they'll figure it out, yeah."

"Congratulate them for me. They did a good job on you."

"Well, thank you, but my mother would have given me hell about that first kiss."

"As well she should. I'd like to hear that—your mother giving you hell. What would she say?"

He considered. "Enrique Carlos Alvarez! Ask for what you want. Don't just take!" The words were unaccented, but carried a subtle hint of Spanish lilt. "May I kiss you, Miss Scott?"

"Certainly not!" she said. "What would you have done if I had slapped you?"

He shook his head. "It would have been a little hard to explain to Danny. I'm sure you would have left a mark."

"You wouldn't have hit me back?"

"No! My God—were you really afraid of me?"

"You are stronger than I am."

"You stood up to me, though. I am so sorry, Jenna."

"All is forgiven," she said and kissed him to prove it.

He took her hand, interlacing his fingers with hers. "Did it ever occur to you I might be afraid of you?"

"No, never. You always seemed so sure of yourself... Were you?"

"I was."

"Why?" She couldn't imagine.

"*Porque eres una mujer tan bella y tan feroz...*" Her high school Spanish was up to the challenge, but he couldn't have known that.

"You wouldn't even let Danny say *gracias* to me and now—what? You don't have the nerve to say 'beautiful' to my face?" He was smiling, amused. "Oh, stop smirking! You know you like it when I'm fierce. That never scared you. You were just afraid I'd get you in trouble."

"No, I was afraid you were too much for me to handle."

"That's exactly how I felt!"

"And then I was afraid I'd blown whatever chance I had with you."

"You came pretty close, Enrique Carlos... Did your mother give you that beautiful name?"

"I was named after my grandfathers. Danny was too—Daniel is Celia's father's name."

She wondered if he realized how often he brought the conversation back to his pride and joy. "What about *your* father?"

"Martín," he said, giving the name all its Spanish flavor. "Daniel Martín—it works in either language. He's a great guy, my dad."

"What does he do?"

"He's a carpenter. A very good one. You should have seen the crib he made for Danny."

"Ah—that's where you learned those skills...and how to treat women?"

"I'm sorry!"

Jenna squeezed his hand. "Your honor, the defendant has demonstrated real remorse. I recommend clemency."

"Thank you. Who were you named after?"

"Nobody. My mother found it in a book. Your family is far more interesting than mine. Tell me more."

He had a firefighter brother—"I won't introduce you; you might like him better than me"—and a sister and didn't want Danny to be an only child. He and Celia had been trying for a girl, but although he remembered every word of the confession, he hadn't wanted to see the autopsy results and didn't know if she was pregnant when she died.

"Oh, Rick, that's so sad," she said, leaning into him. She couldn't understand why he didn't seem to be damaged, scarred by the devastating loss he had suffered. What was the source of his strength? Faith, character, upbringing, work? No, her money was on Danny.

"I'm sorry," he said. "I'm not used to having such a sympathetic listener. Now it's your turn."

Patrick was attractive, in a boyish, black-Irish kind of way. He tended to forget anniversaries but always remembered to pay the bills. He worked long hours, and she hadn't suspected the real reason—until he called her by his assistant's name in bed.

"Stupid bastard," Rick said with feeling. "I hope you decked him."

"No, but I threw a few things. He told me I was crazy and he was leaving me for her."

He shook his head. "Were you happy before you found out?"

"I thought I was—or should be."

"Did you want children?"

"Yes, I did, and he said he did, but we agreed to wait a few years, to be sure we were okay financially. I wouldn't have waited much longer. Now Iris, his assistant—she's pregnant."

"Oh, Jenna! That must have hurt."

"It did, but now I feel sorry for her. She's stuck with him."

"Did you take him to the cleaners?"

"No, all I'm getting is clear title to this place—and my self-respect."

"That doesn't seem fair."

"I didn't want fair. I wanted it to be over."

"When will the divorce be final?"

"March—oh, it's next week."

"Well, that's not so bad." He sounded relieved. Catholic guilt? Or was he afraid Patrick would want her back? "Are you going to celebrate?"

"No, I'm going to ignore the occasion. I'm done." Yes, now she really was.

Presently Rick said he had to do a few things before he picked up Danny and he should let her get some work done, and they parted with a kiss.

Not long after he left, Rosalie returned with fresh gossip and more apologies. "So," she said, "You and Rick…?"

"I don't know," she said honestly. She no longer cared whether Rosalie would repeat everything she said. Sticks and stones had done their worst. "You know, I meant to ask you, before these terrible rumors started, whether he had a reputation for…"

"He had a reputation for doing good work and keeping to himself. I always thought it was a terrible waste, but I guess he was waiting for the right one to come along." It was a waste, Jenna agreed. It also made her feel a great weight of responsibility. Was she good enough, strong enough? Would *she* break *his* heart?

The latest news was that the boys who had been throwing rocks and accidentally broke a window had seen a car near the cabin. If someone had been there before the barbecue, it might or might not be relevant. Their description was vague, but the vehicle wasn't Mrs. Raymond's convertible and it was a car, not a pickup. Vince Allan was looking into it. As for the war coverage on TV, which at Rosalie's was on all day now, the current situation was said to be "withdrawal by disintegration."

"How's Larry?" Jenna asked.

"He'll survive," Rosalie said. "Still spitting mad at you and Rick, though. He'll apologize before I'm through with him. He's grounded for the near future, and all his chore money will go to pay for the paint job. We didn't raise our son to be a vandal. I think Mike was angrier about that than anything else. You know men and their macho pride. He didn't even seem surprised about Mrs. Raymond. It was almost like he already knew.

"I'll tell you the truth—I was a little bit relieved to know it was Larry who was with her. For a while I was wondering if it was Mike… I know I shouldn't say this, and it's just between you and me, but he is sort of a

141

flirt, and it wouldn't have been the first time he strayed. Don't get me wrong—I love the man, and he's been a good husband in every other way. He's always been a good provider. He has a temper, but so do I. His flirting is the only thing we ever fight about."

****

Not until much later, when she was getting ready for bed, did Jenna remember Nancy saying her parents had had a fight. She had refused to go to church with them because they had a fight and then pretended everything was all right. It would have been the same Sunday morning that the body had been found on the rocks, the morning after the barbecue. Had Mike and Rosalie been fighting because he flirted at the party, or because he was out late, perhaps with another woman?

Rosalie had said Mike wasn't surprised, as if he had known about Larry and Mrs. Raymond, which didn't necessarily mean he did know. If Larry had told him, wouldn't he have told Rosalie and the police? Unless Larry had confided in him, man to man, on the condition that no one else would ever know. But promise or no promise, would he have withheld the information when his son was missing?

If Larry hadn't told him, how could he have known? Could a witness have seen Larry there? Who could have told Mike? Nobody else could know what happened.

Except Barbara Raymond.

Something was wrong with her reasoning or Rosalie would have come to the same conclusion. If she even suspected such a thing, she wouldn't have mentioned Mike's flirting to Jenna. Surely it was by such idiotic reasoning that so many people had come to the conclusion that Rick had done it. Still…

She went resolutely to bed, wishing her neighbor had kept her marital problems to herself.

Chapter Twelve

Wednesday, February 27: President Bush declares suspension of offensive combat and lays out conditions for permanent cease-fire.

Jenna woke to the sound of rain on the roof. It was a sweet sound, rare enough to be fully appreciated, and she lay still and warm, savoring it. She was conscious of being alone, and yet she had someone in her life, someone of consequence. He was sending her mixed signals, though. He said he would back off—no, he said he would if she needed him to—and almost immediately took her to bed and then...backed off. Was it up to her to take the next step? Would she?

She had always subscribed to the romantic notion that she couldn't help who she fell in love with, any more than she could keep from tripping and losing her balance. Now she saw clearly that it wasn't true. She might not be able to choose the person she was attracted to, but people didn't fall in love with everyone they were attracted to. She could trip and regain her balance. There was a space of time here in which she could actually make a decision—to resist the attraction, to draw back from the precipice, or to let go and fall—consciously, willingly, wholeheartedly—*into* love.

The rain was coming down hard now, blowing against the window. Now she remembered not only

Rick's comforting presence yesterday but the painful events of the day—Larry coming home in a police car and calling her "stuck-up bitch" and Rosalie confiding that Mike had been known to stray. From that she had somehow come to the conclusion that Mike had guilty knowledge of Barbara Raymond's death. Which he kept from the police and went home and argued with his wife and to church the next morning with his family and behaved normally enough that nobody noticed?

Larry, meanwhile, was "sure mad at somebody" according to Nancy. She wanted to ask Rick's opinion, but Rosalie had said the secret was between the two of them. She would *not* spread gossip.

Rain was still falling when she got up. She showered and dressed and made coffee and toast. Would she see Rick today? She wished he had a phone or she could ease him out of this small-town habit of not making definite plans. She should hope he wouldn't come, that he would be too busy working, earning a living, that the rumors were fading and someone, Violet if nobody else, would hire him to do a substantial job. But she did want to see him. They had talked a lot yesterday, but her mind was full of a million questions she hadn't thought to ask and some she wasn't sure she could ask.

There was a loud knocking at the front door. She hadn't heard the familiar crunch of tires on gravel, but the rain might have masked the sound. She hurried to the door. It was Nancy Hayes, sheltering under a large red umbrella, her pigtails askew.

"Miss Scott," she said in an urgent whisper. "I'm not supposed to be here, but I had to say goodbye. We're going to stay with our Aunt Elaine, me and

Larry. I mean Larry and I. Mom and Dad are fighting again. Everybody's mad because Larry ran away, and he's mad at you because he's so stupid, and I don't want to go, but I won't have to do fractions, and Aunt Elaine is grouchy, but she has lots of books and she lets me read them. I'll tell you all about them when I come back. Oh—and the boring old war is getting over."

"Nancy!" yelled a furious voice, young and masculine, presumably Larry's.

"Stupid!" said Nancy. "Bye, Miss Scott!" and she was gone, running into the rain.

She supposed Mike and Rosalie were wise to send the children away for a little while, and it would certainly be more comfortable for her without Larry's seething anger next door. Nancy had been definite that only the two of them were going. Whatever Mike had known or done, he wasn't running away.

A few minutes later she did hear the sound of the pickup in the driveway, muffled but recognizable. She went to the door. Rick was wearing a jacket but didn't have an umbrella, and he ran up the steps to get out of the rain.

"Hi," she said.

"Hi—I just had a great idea. Where's the—" He strode ahead of her into the kitchen, took the *Scott Kitchen* plan down from the wall, and spread it out on the table. "What if instead of *this,* we changed it so…" He groped for a pencil in his pocket, realized he didn't have one, looked around the kitchen and finally at her.

"Good morning, Enrique," she said.

"Oh, sorry, good morning. Do you have a pencil?"

Jenna wordlessly handed him a pencil and then asked, "Is this what you think about when we're not together—my kitchen?"

"No, but this is what I do, Jenna. This is what I can give you."

"You don't have to give me anything," she said.

"Okay, but give me a break here. It's been a long time since I've done any courting."

"Courting? That's an old-fashioned word."

"I'm an old-fashioned guy."

"Which is not a bad thing," she said. "Take off your jacket. You're dripping." He took it off, and she hung it from the shower rod in the bathroom. When she returned, he had altered the drawing, and yes, she could see it was better, but she couldn't get as excited about it as he had. He was wearing a blue dress shirt, too nice to work in. "What are you dressed up for?" she asked.

He handed the pencil back to her, reluctantly abandoning his brilliant idea. "It's up to you. This weather isn't what I had in mind, but we could still drive to the city and have lunch. I promise I won't make you look at wood or fixtures or anything."

"It's a long drive."

"Yes, but—how did you come into town, on the highway? There's another way, more scenic and only a little longer." She had a distant memory of her grandfather driving along a green-shaded road and telling her it would take them all the way to Carroll City, although they hadn't gone that far.

"Or if you don't want to do that today, I'll get out of your hair and let you work, and you can come to our place for dinner. Danny would love it."

She set aside her concern about setting Danny up for disappointment and asked, out of simple curiosity, "Do you cook?"

"Why?" he asked, sounding a bit insulted. "Does Danny look like he's starving?" No, of course not. Danny was healthy and well-fed, and no doubt Rick cooked meals, probably better than she did, and made school lunches and did laundry and all the other things entailed in being a single father. He didn't need a woman in his life. He didn't need anyone.

Jenna gave him a kiss. "My apologies. Let's hold off on dinner for now. I should work today, but I'm not exactly in the mood, and the light isn't right anyway."

"You're not in the mood? Is something wrong?"

"No, nothing, I'm imagining things. Let's do it— the scenic route, lunch. Should I change clothes?"

He gave her a once-over. "You look great to me," he said. "I like the—uh…"

Jenna shook her head, amused. She was wearing a simple peach cotton-blend dress with a V neck. No doubt the neckline was what he liked. "I'll get a sweater," she said. "If you try the hall closet, I bet my grandfather left an umbrella."

"Umbrellas are for sissies," he said, but he opened the closet door. He sounded happy, relieved—because she had fallen in with his plan for the day or because they were getting out of town? He found a big black umbrella, the old-fashioned kind that required a fair amount of strength to force open. A good, macho umbrella, not for the faint of heart.

"Oh, wait," she said. "If we'll be in the city anyway, let me call in and renew a prescription." One she had allowed to lapse.

"Jim might be able to fill it," he said.

"No," Jenna said. "I think not." She dug into her purse for the slip with the prescription number and picked up the phone. The pharmacy was able to fill the order right away, so that would be taken care of.

"We should stop at Sam's, though," he said as soon as she was off the phone.

She didn't ask what he needed. "Don't go looking for trouble," she warned.

"I never do," he said.

The rain had almost stopped when they walked out to the pickup. Jenna was dubious, ready to suggest they use her car, but the cab was roomier than she had expected, the seat was comfortable, and the door had a padded armrest. "This is nicer than I thought it would be," she said.

"This is a *great* vehicle, babe. They don't make them like this anymore."

"Did you just call me babe?"

"Yeah, babe, I did."

She had to laugh at his tone. "You're in a good mood."

"Yes, I am. I am going out on a date with my best girl in my excellent ride."

"You love this old truck," she said.

"This is not a *truck*. This is a classic Ford Ranger pickup. Have some respect."

"It really hurt to have it vandalized," she suggested.

"Yes, it did," he said. "They'd better do a good job on the refinish. If Danny had done something like that, I would make him strip it by hand, not just pay for it, but I'd rather not let Larry anywhere near it."

"Rosalie was very upset when she saw the vandalism. I wonder if she suspected he had done it."

He didn't answer. They had arrived in the business

district of town, and he parked in front of Sam's Grocery. "Do you want to stay here?" he asked.

"I want you to stay here," she said. "Let's not spoil the mood."

He hesitated briefly, but he got out. She took a deep breath and followed. As they walked into the store, where a group of people were gathered talking near the counter, he took her hand. All conversation stopped. Jenna recognized Gabe Burrows, Megan Wells, and Charlene Dickens, and behind the counter Jim Kelly. She supposed the gossip could now be more about Larry, but they all stared at her and Rick. A large poster on the wall caught her eye:

SATURDAY, MARCH 2
STARTING AT 11 A.M.
BARBECUE AT THE HOPKINS ESTATE
IN CELEBRATION OF THE GULF WAR VICTORY
EVERYONE IS WELCOME.
THOSE WHO STARTED OR KNOWINGLY
SPREAD VICIOUS RUMORS ABOUT A VALUED
MEMBER OF OUR COMMUNITY
ARE NOT INVITED.
YOU KNOW WHO YOU ARE, AND BY
SATURDAY WE WILL KNOW TOO.
VIOLET & DAVID HOPKINS

"Good morning," Rick said to Jim Kelly, who nodded in reply. Rick picked up a bag of nuts from the nearby display and tossed them on the counter. "These are locally grown," he told Jenna. "You can't get them in the city."

The others stood back and waited while they completed the transaction, and then Jim said, "Morning, Jenna."

"Good morning," she managed to reply, still reeling from the impact of Violet's sign.

"You're looking particularly nice this morning," Jim continued. "Isn't she a pretty picture today, folks? Pretty as a blushing bride." He winked at her.

"Oh, jeez," said Gabe Burrows, turning away in disgust. Nobody else spoke.

"Thank you, Jim," Jenna said and let Rick lead her outside. In the pickup, she said, "Did you see the sign?"

"Couldn't miss it," he said and gave her his rare, sweet, dazzling smile.

She smiled back and…let go. She was surprised to discover that it was not much like *falling* in love after all. It was more like flying.

"Do you know Charlene Dickens?" she asked after they pulled away from Sam's.

"I've seen her in church," he said.

"I don't think she'll be at the barbecue. She's pretty toxic. She was the one who said you killed your wife."

"I'll keep that in mind," he said. "Have some of those nuts. They're great."

"They must be, if we had to stop for them," she said. In fact they *were* good, unsalted but meaty and flavorful. She settled back to enjoy the ride. Rick was a careful driver, and she noticed he never took his eyes off the road, no matter how interesting the conversation, a quality she much appreciated. He would not run a stop sign during an argument, as Patrick once had.

It rained on and off all the way, but the road was in good repair and not slick, and the rain only enhanced the scenery, all shining trunks and green boughs. Jenna liked the rhythmic swish of windshield wipers and the intermittent patter of rain on the roof of the car.

"How's Danny doing?" she asked presently.

"Danny is fine," he said. "Danny is a pretty happy kid most of the time. I don't know what I did to deserve him."

"How is Señorita?"

"Fat and sassy as ever. How are you?"

"Happy," Jenna said simply.

The conversation took a serious turn only once. "I know I already apologized for kissing you," Rick said.

"Several times," she agreed.

"But I need to say something else. I was thinking about it last night—I have a lot of time to think when Danny's asleep. I realized it was what you said it was—assault. It seemed like a good idea to me at the time, but in fact it was different only in degree from what those bastards did to Celia."

"Oh, Rick, don't say that! That's a terrible thing to say!"

"Yes, but it's true. I want to make sure you know I'm capable of more restraint than that."

"I know. I noticed."

"Let me finish. I don't want you to be afraid of me ever again. You can always say no to me—always, Jenna. Sooner is better than later, but *always.* If you ever feel like I'm pushing you or you don't like what's happening for any reason—I will stop. And I will never ever hit you, even if you hit me first. Okay?"

"Okay. But I liked the kiss."

"Oh, yeah? You could've fooled me."

"It was your presumption I objected to."

"But you would have slapped me if you hadn't been afraid I'd hit you back?"

"No, I wouldn't have—too melodramatic—but I wanted to."

"Take your best shot—preferably not while I'm driving."

"I'll pass, but while we're on the subject, should I be concerned that the only times we've made love were right after you talked about your wife?"

"What? Seriously?" He was silent for a moment. "No—sorry about the timing, but no. I'm never going to forget Celia, whether I talk about her or not, but what happens between you and me is about you, nobody else... What was your name again?" Jenna didn't laugh. "Oh, come on," he said, "That was a good one...no?"

"No."

"Oh, because your husband—I get it. I'm slow, but I get there eventually. I'm sorry, but here's a news flash for you—I'm not your ex. Okay, it was a bad joke, but don't blame me for what he did."

"I'm not," she protested. "I wouldn't. Are we having a fight?"

"No, no, I'm sorry. I want to do this right. You want anniversaries? We met on February eleventh. You wore blue, which I'd guess is your favorite color. You introduced yourself as Scott, so I assumed you were unattached."

"I didn't mean to mislead you." She examined her ring finger. There was still a faint line, but he wouldn't have looked for it.

"No, of course you didn't. It was none of my business. We didn't meet in a singles bar. You just wanted your roof fixed. I thought you were cute as hell—but you're a lot more than that. I know who you are, Jenna. Trust me. You can take it to the bank. You don't have to laugh at my jokes, though, and if it's too soon for you to be involved, I can live with that. I can wait."

"I think it's too late."

"I didn't mean—"

"I know what you meant." She wasn't ready to say "I love you," but she did love him. He was right; he wasn't Patrick, and she wasn't the terrified girl he had taken to bed on Sunday night. She was *una mujer bella y feroz*, a fierce, beautiful woman. He knew that; he knew who she was. "I wish I had met you first," she said.

"No, no, *querida*, you were too young. You're probably still too young. And I was a basket case."

"After Celia died?"

"What's the quotation—what doesn't kill you makes you stronger? It does, but it takes a while to be sure it *isn't* going to kill you." Jenna put her hand on his on the steering wheel. Even an hour ago she would have bristled at *querida*, told him she wouldn't be called anything he might have used with Celia, but now…what the hell; she liked it.

A few minutes later they stopped at an out-of-the-way gas station, one of the few in California where an attendant still provided basic services. The teenage boy who sauntered out to help them knew Rick but didn't have much to say. They sat in silence while he pumped gas, cleaned the windshield, and made change. When they were ready to leave, Jenna said, "Let's kiss and make up."

"We weren't fighting," Rick insisted.

"Let's pretend we were, so we can kiss and make up."

"Oh, these arduous dating rituals..." They kissed, and his hand lingered on her cheek. "I'm sorry I got upset," he said.

"I'm sorry I didn't laugh at your joke." He kissed her again, and his hand slipped under her skirt to caress her knee, her thigh. It was like high school, but better—the sweet awkwardness of making out in the front seat, but with greater physical confidence and a comforting sense of emotional security. He was not going to break her heart, and he was *very* good at this...

The young attendant yelled, "Get a room!" Laughing, they drove on.

"So you thought I was cute?" Jenna asked. "When we met?"

"Cute as hell," he said emphatically.

"Why?"

"*Why?* Look in a mirror sometime."

"I think you're cute too. You're the cutest boy in town."

"Oh, God," he said. "I'll never live this down, will I?"

"How do you say *cute* in Spanish?" she asked.

"Oh, no, I'm not touching that one. Don't make me sorry I asked you out." She laughed and squeezed his arm. He was so easy to tease, so easy to love.

****

In Carroll City, they started with the large, trendy shopping center, where Jenna could stop at the pharmacy and they could do some window shopping. She was a little disoriented to be in such a busy, crowded place again, surrounded by anonymous people who took no interest in their presence. Newspaper headlines in vending machines shouted WAR'S

CLIMAX and IRAQIS IN FULL RETREAT, but judging by snatches of overheard conversation, basketball scores were of more interest here.

As they headed to the parking lot after she picked up her prescription, she shook her head at the ugliness of the blotches of dark green house paint on the driver's side of the pickup. She wondered how indifferent the strangers around them would be if the lettering had been left uncovered. Would they suppose it a joke, a stupid macho boast?

She pointed to the dents in the tailgate. "How did this happen?" she asked.

"Not in a traffic accident," he said. "Some clumsy oaf…"

"You?" she guessed.

"Not me," he said, "The guy I distracted while he was loading. Where do you want to go now? The choice is yours—whatever you want to look at."

The bookstore was her first thought. It was large and brightly lit, an undreamed of paradise for a young reader like Nancy. "Do you like to read?" she asked.

"When I have time."

"What do you like to read?"

"History, biography, occasionally fiction. How about you?"

"Mysteries mostly," she said. "Dick Francis, Tony Hillerman, John Wyatt Mitchell…"

"I read *The Dictionary Murders*," he said, but didn't show any particular interest in the mystery shelves. "San Ignacio has a library, you know…of course it's only open about three hours a week."

They walked on to the children's section. "You said Danny liked Heather to read to him," she said.

"Don't you read to him?'

"Sure, all the time, and now he's starting to read to me. But I'm not Heather. She does voices and she's—well, she's a girl."

Jenna decided to buy a book as a present for Danny and took Rick's advice on the choice. It was *The Neighborhood Trucker* by Louise Borden, the only book about trucks in stock that he hadn't seen yet. The illustrations even included cement mixers.

Coming out of the bookstore, she remembered to tell Rick about the Hayes children being sent to stay with their aunt and, thinking of Larry's angry voice in the rain, asked, "Did you ever think Larry was right, that I'm a stuck-up bitch?"

"No, I don't think those particular words ever crossed my mind," he said, and for some reason was inspired to stop right there in the parking lot and kiss her, bustling strangers or not. "I think this is going very well for a first date, don't you?" he asked.

Next she spotted an electronics store, where they both might find something of interest. Rick browsed among the cameras, but he was not impressed by state-of-the-art technology, and then Jenna called him over to see the mobile phones. They didn't look like telephones at all but like sleek, modern versions of a child's walkie-talkie. "Look," she said. "This would be perfect for you. You could carry it in the truck and anybody could reach you anytime."

"I don't want anybody to reach me anytime," he said.

"But it would be good for business and for Danny in an emergency. You could turn it off at home if you wanted."

Linda Griffin

"They're expensive," he said, "and they only work around the towers." He took the phone out of her hand and put it back in the display. End of discussion.

On the way back to the pickup, Jenna remembered him saying he would buy her a gun for her birthday—so she could shoot him if he broke her heart. Maybe she should buy him a phone for Christmas. A fair analogy? Yes, because in fact she wouldn't have a gun in the house to save her life, not even now, with a killer on the loose. If he did buy her one, wouldn't he be saying, "Get ready to have your heart broken"? What would she be saying if she bought him a mobile phone? "I need to change who you are"? Okay, no phone. He would have to come around to the idea on his own or not at all.

At a home improvement store, she unbent enough on the subject of kitchen remodeling to agree to look at microwaves. She found a few she might like, and Rick wrote down the measurements, but she didn't buy anything. She was getting used to cooking on her grandmother's old stove.

Rick lingered in front of a jewelry store window. "Don't!" she said sharply.

"I know, I know," he said, "I'm just looking," but before they moved on he had somehow coaxed out of her that she considered large stones vulgar and didn't much care for diamonds—so much for Patrick's rock—and would prefer something more colorful, perhaps a small, exquisite sapphire or amethyst. She wanted to ask if Celia had liked diamonds, but didn't. He was willing to talk about her, but didn't like comparisons. She was learning the rules of this relationship.

They had to have lunch fairly early in order to

158

drive back to San Ignacio before school let out. Jenna's first choice was a Mexican restaurant she had been to before, but people were waiting in a long line to get in. They perused the posted menu to see if it would be worth the wait. Rick said, "This might be okay, but…"

"Your mother makes better tamales," she guessed.

"*I* probably make better tamales," he said. "If you want tamales, I'll make them when you come to dinner."

"Will you teach me how to make them?"

"Sure, if you'll tell me what you put in your French toast."

"Cinnamon, vanilla… We'll make it together sometime."

They opted for Fidelia's, an upscale Italian restaurant known for its hot, fresh bread and seafood ravioli. She was taken aback by the prices, but he didn't seem concerned. He asked if she wanted wine.

"I prefer to keep my wits about me," she said. "I'm out with this very dangerous guy." The bread was indeed delicious, still warm from the oven and so moist it didn't need butter.

When they had ordered—Jenna chose spaghetti marinara, and Rick the famous ravioli—he said, "This is sort of like college—taking a girl out to eat, trying to impress her."

"Wondering if you'll get lucky," she added, because she knew he wouldn't say it. "Did you?"

"What?"

"Get lucky in college."

"I don't kiss and tell," he said.

"Lucky for me," she said, but would she ever know about the other women in his life? "Did you meet Celia in college?"

"No, I met her at work, on my first teaching job. She taught Spanish and English as a second language. When we got married, they wouldn't let us teach at the same school. She was more invested in her students, so I transferred."

"I knew you were a nice guy," Jenna said. "I don't think Patrick would have changed jobs for me."

"Okay, I've had enough of this guy Patrick. Where does he live? Are you sure you don't want me to break his neck?"

"Let's pretend you already did, and we can both forget he ever existed." She mimed zipping her lips. "I won't mention him again."

The food was wonderful. Rick let her try the ravioli—she tasted crabmeat, green peppers, mushrooms, and wine sauce. He smiled at her expression. "You'd better order this next time," he said.

Yes, there would be a next time.

He talked her into dessert—"Just this once. It's our first date"—but he barely touched his blueberry crisp.

Jenna's chocolate chestnut cake melted in her mouth. "I'm going to get fat at this rate," she said. "I knew you were dangerous."

He brushed off her suggestion that they split the bill and paid in cash, tipping generously. "I still owe you," she reminded him. "I may have to file a complaint—my contractor keeps refusing to give me an estimate."

"I'm having a little trouble with the math," he said.

The rain had started again while they were eating. They ran to the pickup, having of course left the umbrella inside it. They left in plenty of time to get

160

back to San Ignacio on schedule, but it rained most of the way, and traffic was slow. The showers finally stopped, but they were running a little late. "I guess we should pick Danny up before I take you home," he said.

Jenna was dismayed, not because she didn't want to see Danny or believed his seeing them together would do any harm at this point, but because their good intentions could be so easily derailed. She couldn't explain her feelings and said only, "I don't want to make any mistakes."

"Don't worry," Rick said. "He'll bounce."

"Will I?" she asked.

"You will," he said. "Don't give him the book—save it for dinner tomorrow." Which sounded as if he'd already begun to plan the entire evening. Now she was curious—she wanted to know everything about him and about Danny, to see where they lived, how they lived—would she see pictures of Celia? Did he have a modern kitchen? Did they eat enough vegetables?

San Ignacio Elementary was a small building, but otherwise resembled every other school she had seen. They were in time—the children hadn't begun to come out yet. When they did, Jenna spotted Danny at once and was surprised by a rush of emotion. She had not seen him since he'd brought her flowers on Monday morning, and so much had happened in between. What an extraordinary thing it was to see the features he shared with Rick in this new light, to discover that strong feelings for a child could come from loving his father, even though she hadn't given birth to him. If she and Rick had a little girl together, would she have those spectacular cheekbones?

Then she noticed what he must have seen at once.

A slender, brown-haired woman in a yellow dress held Danny's hand, and he had, if not a black eye, at least a bruise on his cheek. Had they been irresponsible in leaving town at such a time? Rick got out of the pickup, moving slowly, and now she realized this reaction, which she had also noticed when Danny skinned his knee at the barbecue, was not calmness, but a way of controlling the instinct to be overprotective. She got out too but hung back, not sure of her role here.

The woman, presumably Danny's teacher, greeted Rick coolly. "He was in a fight," she said. "He didn't start it."

"I asked you—" he began.

"I can't be everywhere every minute, Mr. Alvarez." She spoke to him with an exaggerated politeness that suggested a previously contentious relationship. "Both boys were kept in at recess," she went on. "We must remember to use our words, mustn't we, Danny?"

"Yes, Miss Lacey," he said meekly, but he was looking at his father.

"Thank you," Rick said in the same overly polite manner. "I'll take it from here."

As soon as the teacher let go of Danny's hand, Rick got down, eye to eye with his son, and gingerly touched the bruised cheek. Behind Miss Lacey's back, he gave Danny a light, affectionate punch on the shoulder, a masculine gesture of approval. "Look who's here," he said, and Danny looked past him.

"Miss Scott!" he cried and ran straight into her, throwing his arms around her waist. "Are you going to marry us?" he asked.

Jenna was too surprised to speak, and Rick,

smiling, said, "Using his words," and to Danny, "Let's not put the lady on the spot."

Recovering, she said, "I'd marry you in a minute, Danny. I'm not so sure about your dad."

They walked back to the pickup, and Rick said, over Danny's head and so quietly she wasn't sure the boy could hear, "She thinks I'll break her heart, but I won't."

She imitated the punch he had given Danny and said, "Behave yourself."

She would have slid over against the door to make room for Danny, but Rick took him on his lap and fastened the seat belt across both of them. Danny grasped the steering wheel in the approved ten-two position, and Rick put his hands on top of Danny's.

As they drove away from the school, he asked, "What was the fight about?"

"I don't know," Danny said indifferently. "Sean cried."

"When you hit him?"

"He's a crybaby," Danny said. "Are we going to Miss Scott's house?"

"We'll take her home," Rick said. He was smiling. This fatherly pride in such uncivilized behavior was absurd, but she couldn't help feeling a little of it herself. The important thing was that, whatever had happened, Danny wasn't upset.

"You are *such* a dad," she said.

As they approached the house, Danny cried, "Police car!" Indeed, a white patrol car with beacon lights was parked in the driveway next door.

"Oh, no," Jenna said involuntarily.

"What?" Rick asked and took a glance at the car as

he pulled into her driveway.

"I know Vince Allan and Rosalie are friends," she temporized.

"It isn't Vince." He stopped in the turnaround, told Danny to stay in the pickup, and came around to open her door. He studied her with curiosity and concern. "It's Officer Landis. What's wrong?"

"I've been trying all day not to believe Mike Hayes murdered Mrs. Raymond."

"Whoa! Where did that come from?"

"Some things Rosalie told me—in confidence."

"Then don't tell me, but there are hundreds of reasons for Landis to be there. So is that what you think about when we're together—who killed Barbara Raymond?"

"I'm sorry," she said. She didn't think he was annoyed—perhaps he was getting her back for the kitchen crack—but she was sorry to have let ugliness intrude. "It was a great day. Thank you, Rick, I had a wonderful time." It sounded like such a clichéd, classic dating formula, and he gave her a knowing smile. "No, really!" she insisted.

He checked to see if Danny was watching before he kissed her. "So," he said, "are we on for dinner tomorrow?"

"Yes. I'll make dessert—no chocolate."

"Six o'clock," he said.

"I'll be there. Next time, we should try the café in town for cheeseburgers—Danny too." She understood —and knew he understood—that although she couldn't be rushed, she had made a commitment.

This time he didn't glance toward the pickup. She could feel the kiss right down to her toes. "Best first date ever," he said.

The passenger door of the pickup opened. "D-a-a-a-a-d!" Rick gave her a heart-stopping smile and hurried to join his impatient son.

She stood in the driveway, watching, until the pickup disappeared up the shoreline road. Before she could turn back toward the house, a police car passed and turned onto the road to town. She couldn't see who was inside.

****

Monica Kelly was the first to call to tell her Mike Hayes had been arrested for Barbara Raymond's murder. At first, Jenna thought she might be fishing for gossip, but apparently she was motivated by concern for Rosalie. Vince Allan, because of his close friendship with her, had stepped aside and handed the case over to Officer Landis. Her phone appeared to be off the hook. Nobody wanted to disturb her if she didn't want company, but since Jenna was right next door, maybe she could check on her?

Reluctantly she agreed.

"If she wants somebody to stay with her tonight, or if there's anything we can do for her, you'll let us know?"

"Of course." She hung up and stood where she was, unsure what to do next. She didn't even know how to think about this, much less what to do. She remembered Rosalie coming over on her first day here, only a couple of weeks ago, and saying, "You can just walk up anytime." Rosalie had delivered a casserole so she wouldn't have to cook when she was tired from moving in. She could hardly do less.

Obviously Rosalie was the better cook. Rick, who

was so good with his hands, was probably a better cook. "It's the thought that counts," she told herself firmly and surveyed the kitchen for something she could use to make an acceptable offering.

****

Sunset was past when she started up the hill to Rosalie's, but the full moon had risen, and she had no trouble finding her footing. The rain clouds dispersed, but the air remained damp and chilly. She had wrapped the casserole, still warm from the oven, in a dishtowel.

Remembering that nobody in San Ignacio had yet rung her doorbell, she ignored the decorative button beside the Hayes front door and knocked loudly. "Hello?" she called, as Rosalie had done the first day. "Rosalie?"

She waited for a long time and was about to turn away when Rosalie opened the door. She looked weary but calm, her hair slightly disarranged, her plain housedress a little rumpled.

"Jenna," she said without emotion.

"I might be the last person you want to see," Jenna began.

"Nobody blames you for anything," Rosalie said and opened the screen door to let her in. The drapes had not been closed, and no lights were on in the living room, but the TV was blaring.

"I won't stay if you don't want company. I brought you a casserole in case you didn't want to cook tonight. You can just heat it up, or you can put it in the freezer for later. I'm sure it's not as good as yours, but…"

"Thank you," Rosalie said and took the covered dish from her. "It smells good." She had no expression at all in her voice. She stepped into the kitchen, where she put the casserole on the table, and just stared at it. "Should I—?"

"Whatever you want to do. Have you eaten anything?"

"No. Have you?"

"No, but I can—"

"Please stay," Rosalie said in what sounded like a parody of good manners. "I'll…I guess I should…make a salad."

"Let me. You just sit down and rest."

"Rest?" She shook her head, but she sat down at the kitchen table. Jenna set the oven to preheat and rummaged in the refrigerator for salad fixings. While she tore lettuce, Rosalie said, "I know what everybody will say, but I'm going to stand by him."

"Nobody will judge you, whatever you do. Monica asked me to tell you she'll come over if you want someone to stay tonight, or—"

"No. But if you could stay for a while…eat with me."

"Of course."

"He didn't mean to kill her, you know." Oh, no, he just happened to take his fishing knife with him. Doesn't everybody? Gabe was right—Rosalie was too trusting. "She taunted him. She said things about Larry… She wasn't a good woman. She seduced our sixteen-year-old son! She asked for it." Yes, Jenna thought, let's all blame the victim.

When the food was ready, Rosalie didn't want to eat in the dining room, where Mike had so often sat at the head of the table, and they took trays into the living room. Jenna switched on the lights and closed the drapes, but couldn't get Rosalie's consent to shut off the television. She remembered Mike and Larry sitting here, absorbed in the war news, while Rick was being questioned by the police, and had to admit she wasn't as forgiving as Rosalie.

Rosalie took a bite. "What's in this?" she asked with such puzzlement that Jenna couldn't help laughing. "No, it's delicious," Rosalie assured her, managing a faint smile. It did taste pretty good, if not up to Rosalie's standard, and it was at least hot and filling.

On the screen, anchors cheerfully reported that the ceasefire was scheduled for nine p.m. Pacific Standard Time. They showed coverage of the liberation of Kuwait City and reported, in a self-congratulatory tone, the remarkably low Coalition casualty rates. They were gleeful because only about two hundred and fifty American boys had been killed.

"Tell that to the two hundred and fifty families," Jenna said bitterly.

"Why don't you support the war?" A legitimate question, when there had been such an outpouring of patriotic approval.

"Because it's war. But I am sorry I said what I did to Larry. I'm sorry if it led to...all this."

Rosalie shook her head. "Nice to think you're so important," she said. "A few words don't make that much difference. If anybody else is responsible for what Mike did, it's me. If I was a better wife...if I had been enough for him..."

"Don't say that," Jenna said sharply. "This is not your fault. You're a victim too. You were deceived." Hadn't she had the same idea, that Patrick wouldn't

168

have strayed if she had been a better person? Wouldn't she have just had to break up with him later on? He was not the man she was meant to be with.

Rosalie stared at her for a long time before she spoke. "We're all victims," she agreed. "Mike too—but I'm sorry he let Rick take the blame. I don't know why. He did such a beautiful job on the cabinets...and you know nobody would ever want to hurt Danny."

"Danny's fine."

"Mike was just scared, you know, and everybody seemed so willing to believe Rick was guilty. Three years isn't very long in a place like this. Will you tell him how sorry I am?"

"He always knew you were on his side," she said. "You're not responsible." It was easy to forgive, with painful memories—Rick saying "I was blindsided," and KILLER painted on the pickup—fading in importance next to everything she was feeling now.

She stayed until just before nine and walked down the hill in the crisp evening air, knowing the Gulf War was ending. She had distanced herself from it but was deeply grateful it was over and had ended as well as violent conflict ever can. She remembered that the ground war had not even begun when she arrived, and Barbara Raymond was still alive, and she had never heard of Enrique Alvarez. Rosalie had brought her a casserole, and now she had paid back the favor, coming full circle.

Just as she had the first day, she strolled down toward the harbor and wished she had the talent to capture the beautiful, changing ocean—moonlit now, sparkling and mysterious. Her thoughts drifted to anticipation of tomorrow, and she smiled to herself as she headed toward home. Would she meet Señorita, the cat? What would Rick and Danny like for dessert? And after dinner, after dessert, after Danny was in bed…?

In seventeen days, the last seventeen days of a distant war, in this small town, beside this vast ocean, her life had profoundly changed, and this ending was only another beginning.

Afterword

Enrique Carlos Alvarez and Jenna Marie Scott were married on June 23, 1991 in San Ignacio Grace Church. The following year they had a daughter, named Lucia Jane after her grandmothers. They lived in Rick's house while he remodeled Jenna's kitchen and built an addition to the Scott house, where they continue to live happily ever after. Jenna now does her design work on a computer, and Rick carries a cell phone, which he never uses while driving. He still drives a Ford Ranger pickup.

****

Lucia Alvarez graduated from UCLA in 2014. She now teaches in San Ignacio and is engaged to be married. She has auburn hair and her father's cheekbones, loves chocolate, and is fluent in Spanish. She has a cat—or the cat has her.

****

Daniel Alvarez became an engineer, specializing in diesel engines for large trucks. He married his college sweetheart and recently made Rick and Jenna grandparents. He and his family live in Carroll City and visit San Ignacio often.

****

Nancy Hayes became a bestselling children's author and married a local fisherman. Her two most successful novels were set in Nazi Germany. Jenna illustrated Nancy's nonfiction book about the peace movement.

****

Mike Hayes served fifteen years in prison for Barbara Raymond's murder and never returned to San Ignacio. Rosalie divorced him and married Vince Allan after his wife died in 1994. Vince retired in 2006, and they travel extensively. She still loves gossip.

****

Charlene Dickens was convicted of perjury in a 1997 mail fraud case and served eighteen months. She died of cancer in 2002. There was no funeral.

****

One of Celia Alvarez's killers died in prison in 2008. The other is now a born-again Christian and counsels his fellow inmates. Rick has never forgiven them.

****

Patrick Callahan was married three more times and struggles to pay alimony and child support to his second and third wives. He has a serious problem with alcohol and two DUI convictions. Jenna forgave him a long time ago. Rick still thinks he's a stupid bastard.

****

Heather Kelly married Larry Hayes and lives in San Ignacio with their two children. Larry joined the US Army September 12, 2001, and was killed in Afghanistan eight months later. He died a hero.

A word about the author…

Linda Griffin is retired from the San Diego Public Library, and her fiction has been published in numerous journals. In addition to the three Rs—reading ,writing, and research—she enjoys Scrabble, movies, and travel. Visit her at:

www.lindagriffinauthor.com
www.facebook.com/lindagriffin.author
www.twitter.com/LindaGriffinA
www.instagram.com/lindagriffinauthor.